GUN THIS MAN DOWN

OTHER FIVE STAR WESTERN TITLES BY LEWIS B. PATTEN:

GUN THIS MAN DOWN

A WESTERN DUO

LEWIS B. PATTEN

FIVE STAR

A part of Gale, Cengage Learning

GALE
CENGAGE Learning

Detroit • New York • San Francisco • New Haven, Conn • Waterville, Maine • London

GALE
CENGAGE Learning

Copyright © 2010 by Frances A. Henry.
The Acknowledgments on page 209 constitute an extension of the copyright page.
Five Star Publishing, a part of Gale, Cengage Learning.

LIBRARY OF CONGRESS CATALOGING-IN-PUBLICATION DATA

Patten, Lewis B.
    [White Cheyenne]
    Gun this man down : a western duo / by Lewis B. Patten. —
1st ed.
       p. cm.
    ISBN-13: 978-1-59414-909-2 (hardcover)
    ISBN-10: 1-59414-909-7 (hardcover)
    1. Western stories. I. Patten, Lewis B. Gun this man down. II.
Title.
PS3566.A79W46 2010
813'.54—dc22   2010019570

First Edition. First Printing: September 2010.
Published in 2010 in conjunction with Golden West Literary Agency.

Printed in the United States of America
1 2 3 4 5 6 7 14 13 12 11 10

TABLE OF CONTENTS

★ ★ ★ ★ ★

THE WHITE CHEYENNE

★ ★ ★ ★ ★

I

Julien Tremeau awoke suddenly that morning, wondering at once what it was that had wakened him, and what caused the instant apprehension that touched his mind.

Beside him lay Bird Woman, her gentle face relaxed in sleep. Above him was the weathered hide covering of the lodge, cured by smoke, familiar and friendly. Across the robe-strewn floor slept the children, Black Feather, a boy of seven, and Little Bird, a girl of five. Between them, warming them protectively, slept Night Star, sister to Bird Woman, who Julien had taken as his second wife, though her position in the lodge had never been truly that of a wife.

Julien Tremeau. That was his name among the whites. Here, among the Cheyennes, it was Black Dog. But was he Indian or white? Neither, and both, he thought, as he lay here this wintry morning with his Indian family around him.

His breath billowed out above him, a cloud in the frosty air. The fire in the center of the teepee had died to a bed of gray coals.

Still apprehensive, still puzzled as to the cause of it, he stirred and eased himself from beneath the warmth of the robes. Bird Woman opened her eyes, looked at him, and immediately rose silently to join him. Her eyes were wide as they studied his face. "What is it, Black Dog?" she asked in the Cheyenne tongue. "What troubles you?"

He shook his head, having no answer for her, indeed having

no answer for himself. He reached for his rifle, tomahawk, and knife. Once more his glance swept the teepee. And then he stepped outside.

It was a gray morning. High, thin clouds overlaid the blue of the winter sky, as yet untouched by the morning sun. Snow lay in patches on the north side of the low, rounded hills. The ground underfoot was frozen hard.

A few others were up and out, mostly early-rising squaws. Without exception they were gazing toward the bluff behind the village. Without exception their dark faces showed startled, growing fear.

Julien's head swiveled to follow their glances. His body stiffened and his hands tightened involuntarily on the rifle. His eyes, gray as the ashes of a dead fire, narrowed almost imperceptibly.

Tall he was, this son of mountain man Charles Tremeau, tall and strong and bronzed of skin. In coloring he favored his Cheyenne mother. In dress and bearing he could not have been distinguished from any other Cheyenne brave. But those gray eyes . . . and the expression they held. . . .

Education put that indefinable expression into a man's eyes. And knowledge. Here was one, they said, who had gone to the white man's schools. Here was one who had lived the best of the white man's life. Here, too, was one who had chosen, and who would never regret the choice.

Up there on the bluff. . . . His heart told him what the presence of all those soldiers meant. Else why did they appear like ghosts in the cold, thin light of dawn? And why, with no warning, with no sound to betray their presence?

He wanted to shout, to bellow out the alarm. But his lips seemed locked.

Some of the squaws began to cry out with alarm, warning the braves of the camp. Teepees began to spew their occupants into

10

the frosty morning air.

Fear was a growing, tangible thing in this village of Black Kettle on the bank of Sand Creek. And behind Black Dog, behind this Julien Tremeau, the occupants of his own lodge stirred and awakened with querulous questions on their lips.

Cannon there on the ridge, waiting with gaping mouths. Cannon and what looked like a thousand men.

The white trader, Smith, came out and several squaws ran to him, pleading with him to go talk to the soldiers. From the pole in front of Black Kettle's lodge, the stars and stripes of the American Union, beneath it the chief had raised a white flag, to signify truce, or surrender.

Yet even with this, no reassurance touched the mind of Julien Tremeau. Up on the ridge were men of his own race. He knew what was in their minds.

Black Kettle's strong voice rang out across the camp, telling his people not to be afraid. "The whites are our friends. They have come to make peace. The Long Knives at Fort Lyon, at Big Timbers, on the Arkansas, have guaranteed us their protection."

Smith started up the rise. Tremeau saw an arm raise on the ridge. He heard a bellowed command.

Cannon mouths belched black powder smoke. Grapeshot whipped the clustered teepees below. Sound rolled down the bluff in its wake, like thunder on a summer day.

More smoke, but smaller puffs. Rifles. Their spiteful crack blended in a racket more terrible, even, than that of the cannon had been.

No warning. No parleying. Just attack, and murder so cold-blooded it would chill the heart of the most hardened of men.

Unreal—like a dream—like a nightmare from which he must soon awake. A score of feet away a squaw sank to the ground, her hands clutching her torn breasts while blood leaked redly through her fingers.

The cannon boomed again. Grapeshot rattled like hail against the cured hide coverings of the lodges. Children screamed hysterically, with both terror and pain.

Not the children of Julien Tremeau. Not yet. From frozen immobility he sprang into action. He flung aside the flap of the teepee and with a sweep of his great right arm sent both Night Star and Bird Woman sprawling to the floor. "Down!" he roared in Cheyenne. "Down on the ground! Stay until I come for you!"

He leaped back out. He saw a form detach itself from the soldiers on the bluff. Another. They ran down the slope toward the village, tearing at their clothes. One of the Bents. And another, who Julien recognized as Sharp Knife, a white raised by the Arapahoes.

Tearing off the clothes that made them white they ran into the village and disappeared among the teepees there.

On the bluff, the soldiers broke. Down the slope they streamed, kneeling, firing, getting up, and coming on. Bellowed commands by their officers went unheeded as they submerged themselves in a frenzy of murder and death.

Fury—consuming fury greater than any he had ever known before—burst full-grown in Tremeau's brain. He realized that his rifle was empty and hot in his hands. He flung it away. He seized the tomahawk at his belt. And the knife.

He hesitated, on the brink of charging toward the oncoming soldiers. Protect his family—or attack those who threatened them?

He hesitated but for an instant. Then, running like a startled deer, he broke away, charging straight into the oncoming ranks of men.

Behind him, before their teepees, stood the chiefs. Left Hand, chief of Arapahoes, waiting to die, only to be knocked off his feet by the charging body of Sharp Knife, seeking to save his life. White Antelope, arms folded, singing the death chant of the prairie tribes. Black Kettle, mindful of his responsibility, shouting to his people to flee.

A nightmare of horror, bursting over this peaceful village. For these were the ones who did not, who never had, threatened the safety of the whites. The peaceful ones, women old and young, children, old men, and a few of the younger ones who saw the futility of war against the unconquerable tide of whites.

Now they fought. Boys, screaming, charged the advancing, disorderly line of whites. Women did the same. Julien Tremeau clubbed a white soldier with his tomahawk and heard it crush his skull. A man gone wild. Coups he had counted in battle with the Shoshones, but he had never killed a man. Now he killed three in a space of as many minutes.

A rifle roared almost in his ears. The heavy ball tore through the muscles of his left arm. Blood poured down it and ran from the tips of his fingers. And the hand was useless, releasing involuntarily the knife it held.

Not so the other. He flung the tomahawk with deadly accuracy. The stone head buried itself in a soldier's face and the man went down, unrecognizable in the destruction it left in its wake.

Julien Tremeau leaped to recover it. A clubbed rifle knocked him down. He crawled toward his tomahawk. A bullet tore into his leg.

He kept crawling, the screams of the wounded and dying like a dirge of death in his ears. A little girl, blinded with blood, ran toward him, tripped over him, and fell. Bullets tore into her body and she was still at last.

His own family—must they meet this same fate? Was there no stopping it, no turning it back? He must reach them and help them escape.

He recovered his tomahawk. They were all around him now,

these blood-mad whites. A wildly disorganized mob, crazed with hate, inflamed by every tale they had ever heard of Indian outrage. They were even shooting down their own.

Tremeau, crawling, crushed the skull of a wounded soldier with the tomahawk. His left arm dragged limply, brokenly at his side. His brain was afire with pain and shock.

He heard a screeching voice—a voice screaming epithets in English, for there is no profanity in the Cheyenne tongue. It was his own voice, he realized with dull wonder. His own, and the English curses, by confusing the soldiers, had helped keep him alive thus far.

But he couldn't stand. And he had but one good arm.

From the ground, from the welter of blood in which he lay, he flung his tomahawk one last time, knowing that now he could not help his family live. Even as it left his hand, a bullet tore into his chest and passed on through.

The sky was suddenly black. All was quickly silent in his ears. Consciousness was no more. For Julien Tremeau the massacre at Sand Creek was over and done.

Through the village the soldiers passed, pursuing those that fled, downing them with clubbed rifles, with deliberately murderous bullets, with anything that came to hand.

Mutilated bodies lay strewn in their wake, like dolls broken by a cruel and petulant child. For the wounded to move or make a sound was to die.

Only when they had passed did Bird Woman venture from the lodge. Her eyes were stunned, her face white with shock. Forgetting the children, forgetting everything but her consuming love for Julien Tremeau, she ran like a deer toward the bluff, knowing this was the direction her husband would have gone.

Searching—searching among the scattered bodies of the dying and the dead. The noise of horror was in her ears—the callous yells of the white soldiers—the sound of their guns.

Mercifully the cannon were silent now. They could not be fired into the mêlée without killing some of their own.

On through the village passed the soldiers, pursuing survivors. Out to its edge and past ran Bird Woman until at last she found her husband, lying as though dead a hundred yards beyond.

The bodies around him told her he had fought well and had made them pay for his life. Yet she had no eyes for this—only for him, pale and broken on the ground, lying in his own blood.

She fell to her knees beside him. She felt the faint beat of his strong heart beneath her own trembling hands.

The world, which had ended for her with the discovery of his body, began to live again. She looked around frantically. He had to have help. Somehow the bleeding had to be stopped before his life all leaked away.

Her eyes encountered some stragglers, crossing the field toward her. They had seen her, she realized, and now there was no help for Black Dog, no help for his wife.

She glanced around for a weapon. The whites would discover that not only Cheyenne men could fight. Their women could fight as well. And their children, if need be.

A rifle. A soldier's rifle was lying fifteen feet away. She stumbled toward it.

One of the soldiers knelt, taking careful aim. He fired. The bullet struck Bird Woman's body, jerking it half around. She would never reach that rifle now. She was dying on her feet. But in dying, perhaps she could yet save the ebbing life of Black Dog.

Falling, she made a supreme effort, and forced herself toward the body of her husband. She sprawled across it, covering it with her own, concealing the faint rise and fall of his shattered chest.

And the soldiers passed, more interested now in souvenirs and loot than in mutilating the body of a lone woman and an already mutilated man.

Bird Woman, with her last dying thoughts, prayed wordlessly—to the God of Julien Tremeau, who she thought a harsh God, but in whom Julien believed. She prayed as well to the god of the Cheyennes, Heammawihio, who was a wiser, gentler god. And with this prayer on her paling lips, she breathed her last and laid forever still.

Down along the creek the battle raged. Many of The People fled. Others dug pits in the sandy soil beside the creek, and from these pits made their last desperate stand. Not because they hoped to win, but to delay the advance of the white murderers, to give those who had escaped the necessary time to get clear.

Eighty miles to the north and east was camped a larger group than this had been. Eighty miles, that the soldiers would not march even if they dared. For the next attack could not be another surprise attack at dawn. The next would truly be a battle, since the village at Smoky Hill would have been forewarned.

The noise dimmed slowly as the fighting moved farther and farther up and down the banks of the frozen stream. A couple of dozen soldiers prowled the village, finishing off survivors and wounded, searching the teepees for loot.

And in the teepee of Black Dog, Night Star crouched behind a pile of dried buffalo meat stored in rawhide bags. Little Bird and Black Feather crouched, trembling, beside her. They could only wait.

II

Night Star could not know what had happened, either to Black Dog, or to her sister Bird Woman. She could only guess.

They were both dead. Everyone was dead—save for herself and the two small children of Black Dog who she had loved with all her heart, and her sister who she had also loved, but in a different way.

The children must live, and in living give immortality to the two who had died to save them.

Night Star was a small girl, several inches shorter even than her sister had been. She was slender, willowy, and strong as a slim reed growing out of the riverbank.

Her skin was smooth, her eyes warm and soft. She was a wife, and yet not a wife, for never had Black Dog held her in his arms. Nor had he ever treated her as a wife. She was more like a younger sister to him. Except in her heart. There, she had not been like a sister to him.

Now she could never know the ecstasy of lying in his arms. She could never know the joy of possessing and being possessed. She would die, as Black Dog had died, but more slowly, more painfully. She was pretty even by white standards. She knew this because white men had always looked at her with burning eyes.

They would use her brutally before they killed, for such was the way of men with the women of the enemy. This she had been taught.

She looked down at the gleaming knife she held in her hand. Perhaps. . . .

Her eyes lighted. There might be a way. Finding a young woman here, alone, might take their minds away from whatever else might be hidden in the teepee. If she fought, but not too hard, they might completely overlook the children if they were hidden well.

Quickly she covered the children with a robe, cautioning them in whispered Cheyenne to complete silence. She piled rawhide bags of cured buffalo meat around and over them, then she crept closer to the entrance flap and covered herself, but not completely, with another quill-decorated buffalo robe. And now she waited, trembling with fear, a knife in her hand.

Never had Night Star been called upon to show much courage, but she would today. All the courage she possessed would be needed to sustain her in the hours to come.

Voices approached the teepee flap. Their hated voices—their hated, unpleasant words. English, upon the lips of Julien Tremeau, had never been ugly. But it was ugly now, the way these two spoke it.

One said: "Nobody's been in here, looks like. Maybe. . . ." He began to chuckle. "Well, now. Looky what you an' me's found us. A wench. A young 'un too, from the looks of 'er foot stickin' out from under that buffler robe."

For an instant there was silence. Night Star trembled uncontrollably, wondering if, now that the time was at hand, she would have the courage. To endure while life lasted. To die when the enduring was done.

The robe was snatched from her. She felt the brutal impact of a heavy, smelly body as it dived upon her.

She struggled, resolution gone, and tried to bury the knife in the odorous body that smothered her.

It was twisted savagely from her hand, with a wrench that nearly broke her arm. The one who held her snarled: "You god-damn' little bitch! Knife me, will you? I'll show you a thing or two, by God!"

The other, standing, laughed obscenely. "Quit beefin' an' git it over with. She's a pretty one. I want my turn before some god-damn' officer shows up."

Holding her down with the weight of his body across her and with one powerful hand, the bearded one who had captured her began to rip the clothing from her with the other. She struggled, wild with terror. She sank her teeth into his corded, dirty neck.

He howled, jerking away convulsively. Night Star tasted blood. The man swung a clenched fist that struck her in the mouth and brutally snapped back her head. Her consciousness slipped.

The man growled: "God damn it, Jack, hold her. I'm goin' to beat the livin' hell. . . ."

Night Star heard a whimper from one of the children. She knew she must draw these men away—now—before they heard it, too.

She made her tense, trembling body go limp. She ceased to fight. And as she had known he would, the surprised white man relaxed his grip on her.

Instantly she twisted away. She leaped for the flap of the lodge.

Harder than he intended, perhaps, the second man swung at her. And his blow struck her like a club, on the side of her head just above the ear. It was like a star, exploding in her mind. There was a white, dazzling light. There was red, like the blazing evening sun as it sets. And then there was only night.

She fell, half in and half out of the teepee. Her captor, the smelly one she had bitten, rubbed his bleeding neck furiously as he stepped outside. He aimed an angry kick at her, and it struck her in the ribs. "God-damn Injun bitch," he growled. "Jack, gimme my gun."

"You goin' to kill her?"

"Why not? Chivington said no prisoners, didn't he? She'll have a dozen Injun pups afore she's through."

He heard a whimpering from inside the teepee. Forgetting his gun for the moment, he turned back inside. He began to kick aside robes, and at last reached the pile from which the sounds emerged.

Kicking the bags aside, he stooped and whipped the robe from the two children. Immediately Black Feather, the boy, leaped up. There was a small toy tomahawk in the boy's hand. He launched himself at the man, his face twisted with fear, and struck savagely with the tomahawk.

It hit Jess Durand's chest with an audible thump. He seized the boy, upended him, and held him dangling by both ankles. He swung him toward the stones that made up the hearth in the center of the teepee.

The boy's brains would have been dashed out on the hearth, but for the sudden, restraining hands of Jack Ludens. "Hold it! I just got me an idea."

"Idea, hell! This 'un will be murderin' white settlers in another dozen years."

"No. Listen. I got me a carnival over at Denver. Supposin' if, along with a bunch of Injun scalps an' trophies, I had two live Injuns, too?"

"How'n hell would you get 'em there?"

"I'll just get a couple of horses an' take 'em there. You can cover for me, can't you? All you got to do is holler out for me when they call the roll."

"Why'n hell should I? I don't owe you nothin'."

Jack Ludens fished in his pocket. He brought forth a $10 gold piece, a half eagle. "This a good enough reason?"

Jess nodded. The half eagle changed hands. Eagerly now, Jack said: "Keep 'em here an' keep 'em quiet. Tie 'em up whilst you're waitin'. I'll go get me a couple of horses."

He disappeared out the teepee flap. Jess found some rawhide strips and tied the boy's hands and feet. He slashed off a piece of buffalo robe and crammed it in the struggling boy's mouth. Then he bound and gagged the cowering, trembling girl in similar fashion. When he had finished this, he dumped each of them into a buffalo robe, afterward tying the opposite corners of the robes, and then tying them together.

As he was finishing, Jack Ludens returned. He picked up one of the tied bundles and Jess picked up the other. They carried them outside and flung them over the back of one of the horses Ludens had brought. They balanced nicely and looked like loot rather than what they were. Jack swung to the back of one of the horses, holding the reins of the other in his hand. "So long, Jess. There's another half eagle waitin' for you if you get me half a dozen scalps."

And then he rode away.

Scalps. Jess glared down at the Indian girl. He took his knife from its sheath at his belt and ran a finger along its edge. He knelt and seized her hair.

She was breathing, and pale. Her small breasts rose and fell regularly. Jess's eyes brightened and he licked his lips.

Suddenly, decisively he sheathed his knife. There were other scalps to be had. And this one—maybe later when things had quieted some. . . .

He dragged her into the teepee. He flung two or three robes over her. She'd be out for a long, long time. She'd keep.

Picking up his rifle, he went out of the teepee just as a couple of others flung back the flap to enter. He growled: "Nothin' in there, boys. Somebody's beat us to it."

He watched them move away, and moved away himself, searching for scalps among the bodies that littered the ground. He knelt beside a brave, his knife in hand.

He had no time to rise or dodge, no time to plunge the knife into the warrior's chest. He felt the Indian's knife slide between his ribs, and knew a shock of horror. This couldn't be happening! It couldn't! The Indian hadn't been breathing at all.

Unbelievingly he stared at the knife protruding from his chest. He got uncertainly to his feet, staggered a few steps, and sat down. He pulled out the knife and dazedly watched the fountain of blood that followed it. Then, he toppled from his sitting position.

There was little pain. Only shock, growing weakness, and death.

Night Star regained consciousness slowly. She felt smothered by the robes. She wondered if this were death, this darkness, this feeling of airlessness. Then, dimly, she heard sound, and knew she was still alive. Cautiously she wriggled clear of the robes and peered around the lodge. The children were gone. She was all alone.

She could hear shouting voices down toward the creek—the voices of the officers trying to restore some semblance of order to their men. She crept from the teepee flap on hands and knees.

Nothing moved in the village. Nothing that she could see. But she had to get away from it, somehow. She had to find Black Dog, or Bird Woman, or the children. She knew the soldiers would burn the village when they left.

Weakness assailed her. Her head felt light, and hurt terribly. Nothing, compared to the hurts probably sustained by those lying around her. She gazed at their bodies in horror. But she went on, creeping along the ground because she feared she could not stand and yet retain her consciousness.

She reached the edge of the village. Here, the effects of the blow with which Jack Ludens had struck her robbed her of consciousness again. For a long time she lay on the frozen ground, looking as dead as any of the others.

At intervals, she regained consciousness, only to lose it again. Each time she did, she would crawl a little farther, always searching among the bodies of the dead.

She found the two she sought a little before noon and rolled Bird Woman's body from that of Black Dog to discover he was still breathing.

Afterward, working from a prone position, she stanched the flow of his blood with pieces of her clothing and with mud, now thawing under the noonday sun. She fainted frequently. But each time she came to, she would resume her ministrations to Tremeau.

Though she could not know it, she had sustained a severe concussion when Ludens struck her. To recover from it, she needed sleep, and rest, and time. Meantime, her will and her prayers, and her help, kept the spark of life glowing faintly in Julien Tremeau.

The afternoon slipped away. Chivington and his officers called off the pursuit and gathered their scattered forces. There was a camp of Arapahoes on the Arkansas. There was still time to surprise and annihilate them before the enlistments of his one-hundred-days volunteers expired. Still time for a little more glory. . . .

They marched away triumphantly, dragging their cannon, carrying their wounded and their dead. They left behind only a few who lived, who still clung feebly to life, among these Night Star and Julien Tremeau.

Wolves prowled the land that night, quarreling and tearing at the bodies of the dead. The bitter cold increased. Night Star covered the body of Julien Tremeau with her own to keep it warm. And doggedly hung on. Waiting. For help that might not come at all.

III

Charles Tremeau was at Bent's Stockade on the Purgatoire the day before the attack. He saw the army of Chivington arrive and stop briefly across the river from the fort. He suspected their destination and immediately prepared to leave. Julien and Julien's family were with the Cheyennes on Sand Creek. They must be warned, in case this army's objective was that very camp.

It probably was, he knew. It could hardly be another. Except for a small camp of Arapahoes a few miles away, there was no other short of the one at Smoky Hill River.

Tremeau was a tall old man, white of hair, dark of skin. His face was like cured leather above the white, trimmed beard. His eyes were blue and sharp, and very watchful.

He'd wanted more for this son of his than a life among the Cheyennes. There was good about it, surely. There was freedom such as white men seldom knew. There was excitement, and there were the peaceful times as well, when winter froze the streams and blanketed the land with snow. A man could feel content when his children were fat and smiling, when his teepee was well stocked with dried food and meat.

Yes, Charles Tremeau, who had known no other life for thirty years, still knew touches of nostalgia and longing whenever he remembered his own youth in the green, rich farmlands of the East. So when Julien was ten, Tremeau had sent him East, where he had stayed until the year he was nineteen.

Money had never been a problem with Tremeau. The land had treated him well. He had trapped, and sometimes he had panned the streams for gold. He had traded with the Indians, with the Spanish in Santa Fe.

Back East, Julien had seen the best of the white man's life. But in the end he had come back here, to exchange his broadcloth suit, his ruffled shirt, and beaver hat for the deerskins of his Cheyenne friends. To exchange the soft, white girls he had known in the East for a single, strong, brown-skinned girl.

Tremeau saddled two horses and rode to the gate, where a squad of soldiers stood on guard. He started to ride through, only to have them block his way.

"Where the hell do you think you're goin,' old man?"

Tremeau flushed angrily. "Same place I've been goin' for fifty some odd years! Wherever I god damn please!"

"Uhn-uh. Nobody rides out of here tonight. Orders of Colonel Chivington."

For an instant Tremeau hesitated, eyeing the open country beyond the gate. He could make a run for it.

Something of his thoughts must have shown in his eyes, for the corporal raised his rifle. "Don't do it. I got orders to shoot anyone that tries."

Tremeau turned back, apprehension growing in his mind. There could be but one reason for the guard. Chivington feared that news of his objective would leak out.

Tremeau unsaddled and put his horses into the corral. He climbed to the top of the wall and peered over. There were two armed men at each corner, and others walking posts along the walls.

Tremeau's mouth twisted. He could get over and away as soon as darkness fell. But without a horse. And without one, he would be totally unable to reach the Sand Creek camp in time.

Still, he had to do whatever he could. And maybe once outside he would be able to find a horse. An Indian pony. A mule. Anything would do.

The light faded slowly from the sky. Uneasiness was rampant inside the stockade, but the soldiers on guard seemed to know no more about their colonel's destination than did the men inside.

At first full dark, Tremeau waited until the guard had passed, then slid down a rope to the ground outside the fort. On silent, moccasined feet, he slipped away. The guard made half a dozen trips past the dangling rope before it was even seen. By that time, Tremeau was safe, half a mile away.

But he was far behind the troops. And traveling slower because he was afoot and lame from a Pawnee arrowhead. He hobbled away swiftly, to north and east, pushing harder than he ever had before. He picked up the trail of Chivington's hundred-day volunteers and followed it because the going was easier where they had already trampled down the snow. Used to walk-

25

ing this endless land, he could match their pace, but he could not, however hard he tried, gain on them.

The night hours wore away. For every mile he walked, apprehension—fear for his son and his son's family—grew in his worried mind. The direction—toward the Sand Creek camp— the guard around the stockade—the forced night march—these things could mean only one thing. Chivington was going to attack at dawn, without warning, the Sand Creek camp itself.

He plowed through a shallow lake rather than lose time skirting it. And went on.

Dawn lightened the sky and the trail he followed. Studying it, he judged that the soldiers were now several hours ahead of him.

A sound like thunder rolled from the horizon ahead, and then was gone. Cannon. The attack had begun.

Charles Tremeau pushed even harder, his faded blue eyes as hard as bits of stone. His mouth was a grim, straight line. What manner of man was this Chivington, and who had given him his orders to attack the camp?

Yet even the imagination of Charles Tremeau, who had seen suffering and death every year of his life, could not supply an accurate description of the carnage taking place. Even Charles Tremeau could not envisage the wholesale slaughter, the awful mutilation being performed by men who claimed to be civilized.

Now he cursed his age, cursed the Pawnee who had, three years before, put an arrow into his thigh. He hurried on.

Midmorning. The rifle shots were plain now, though scattered and sporadic. He topped a rise and looked down into the village of Black Kettle.

His weathered face turned pale. There was nothing left, nothing but the teepees. The People were gone. Five hundred—six hundred. He didn't know how many. Dead. Wounded. Fleeing across the snowy plain. Only a few soldiers prowled the village, like carrion-eaters feeding off the dead.

Tremeau got up and started down the slope. He looked at the loads in his rifle as he walked, at the loads in the revolver at his belt. And then he stopped. He could kill, before they brought him down, no more than half a dozen of Chivington's men.

But if he waited, if he waited until they were gone, he could save a dozen, a score, of Indian lives if he did no more than build the fire that would keep them warm. Reluctantly he returned to the top of the hill and lay down to wait.

The day dragged on. Suffering was no stranger to Charles Tremeau. Yet his heart grew sick, listening to the moans, the helpless, pitiful cries of the wounded down below. His face twisted as he watched their feeble attempts to crawl away to safety, or to help another do so.

Occasionally, off to the north, he would spot a small group of survivors as they fled toward Smoky Hill, as they topped a low ridge that happened to lie along their route.

Pray God that Julien, and Bird Woman, and Night Star and the children were among those lucky few. Pray God that Julien yet lived.

Night, and at last the troops were gone, silent and exhausted by their day of slaughter. Charles Tremeau walked down from the hill and entered the village.

He built a fire first, a huge fire that could be seen a long way off. It would draw in those still able to travel. Then he began to search for those who, though appearing dead, still lived.

He carried three children, one by one, to the fire. He helped a young squaw who had regained consciousness and had begun to scream. He did all he could with the materials at hand. He fed the wounded meat from a huge pot he had put on to boil at the edge of the fire. And he continued his search, carrying a blazing pine knot in his hand for light.

At last, he found his son, covered by the unconscious body of

Night Star, his second wife. He carried Julien to the fire first, Night Star immediately afterward. He examined Julien's wounds in the orange light of the fire, amazed that the young man had lived this long. His chest still rose and fell, however faintly. His heart still pulsed in his chest.

All through the night, Charles Tremeau worked. And all through the succeeding days, until help from Smoky Hill arrived. He was ill himself when it did arrive, ill with exposure and exhaustion. And so, on the long trek northward, he went along, lying weak and feverish and sometimes delirious on a jolting, swaying travois behind a slowly plodding horse.

The first impressions of consciousness were, to Julien Tremeau, the joltings of the travois on which he rode. They were vague and fleeting impressions, for his widely spaced periods of consciousness were short. He remembered nothing of how he had been hurt, remembered nothing of his family or of the camp on Sand Creek. Life was, for him, a tenuous thing that might evaporate suddenly at any time.

There were periods when he seemed to dream—or perhaps they were not dreams at all, but memories, returned to haunt a barely conscious mind. The early years—the boyhood years, poignant with new experiences never to be forgotten.

He was almost wholly Indian, those first few years. He played with the Cheyenne children at games all children play. He slid down icy hills on sleds made from the rib bones of the buffalo, rode stick horses to the hunt, shot arrows at imaginary Shoshone enemies with a small toy bow.

Charles Tremeau was often absent during those early years, trapping for beaver, panning the mountain streams, guiding wagon trains of supplies and trade goods along the Santa Fe Trail.

"More Indian than white," his father had grunted when he

returned for the winter when Julien was ten. And he was. He rode as well as any of his Cheyenne friends. He had already killed his first game, a deer, and was looking forward with shining eyes to his first buffalo hunt.

He spoke the Cheyenne tongue better than he spoke his own, though his father had always tutored him in basic subjects during the winter's enforced time of idleness.

"I'm gonna send that nigger East," his father had told his mother. "Time he learned. . . ." He had stopped, suddenly, staring at his wife, who was watching him with softly smiling eyes. "Well, anyhow, I'm goin' to send him East. He's half white, though I swear to God you couldn't tell it by lookin' at him."

And so, that year, Julien had said good bye to his friends and traveled East in company with his father. He learned to wear the uncomfortable clothes that white boys wore. He learned to sit in a classroom, quietly and without too much protest, when he would rather have been outside. He even learned to tolerate the thin-lipped, sharp-tongued sister of his father, who kept him with her in her monstrous three-story frame house surrounded by farmland and countless great cottonwood trees.

Hardest of all, he learned not to yearn for the old life in such a way that his yearning was visible, for he soon discovered that the way to remain in the good graces of his aunt was to simulate, at least, a certain degree of civilization.

And so, the long years passed. There were many good things about the white man's way of life, he discovered as he grew. Boys are much the same, wherever they are, whatever they do. They swam in the river shallows and hunted snakes and frogs and toads in the marshes below the town. They walked across the fields, climbed the gnarled old trees, or fished in the farm's small pond.

Julien spun them yarns about the wild, free life of the plains until nostalgia grew so strong he could no longer bear even to think of the plains. The longing was like a pain in his heart.

His aunt died when he was sixteen and he moved into a boarding school. And now, released from his aunt's restraint, he discovered girls, and liquor, and gambling.

He was booted out of school twice for drunkenness. He was nearly horsewhipped by the irate father of a pregnant girl, who controlled himself barely in time when he noticed the odd little gleam in Julien's eyes, the strange, fierce set of his mouth.

At last, when Julien was nineteen, he could stand it no more. The city and its people were crowding in on his mind, changing his whole character. And so, with only the suit on his back and the money in his pocket, he set out for the plains, for the life and the people he loved.

The trail was long, but he loved it, every mile. He was taller. His shoulders were broad, his chest deep and strong. His face, though not as dark as that of an Indian, nevertheless bore many Indian characteristics. High cheek bones and slightly hollow cheeks. The long, strong nose of the Plains Indians. The hard and piercing eyes. A man men left alone. A man they watched, as though trying to fathom him.

He rode from Independence all the way to Bent's Fort with a wagon train of supplies. He arrived, unrecognized, in May of 1855, only to find that his father and mother were out on the plains to the north and east, following the buffalo herds.

And so, without a guide and alone, he rode out, dressed now as an Indian brave and riding an Indian horse. His hair was growing but was not yet long enough to braid. His skin was as bronzed as that of any Cheyenne.

The land lay before him and around him, empty and vast and covered with grass and game for as far as the eye could see. The sky was blue and cloudless over his head, the air soft and warm with the coming of spring.

This, he knew, was the land he loved, the life he loved. He

would live no other. Julien Tremeau had made his choice. He was home at last.

IV

Five days after the massacre, the pitiful caravan arrived at the Cheyenne village on Smoky Hill River, eighty miles northeast of the ravaged village on Sand Creek. News of their coming had preceded them, and The People turned out to welcome and take them in.

Still only fleetingly conscious, Julien was taken into the lodge of Gray Wolf, a middle-aged Dog Soldier, and his three wives. Night Star, recovered now, accompanied him.

Installed in the warmth of the lodge, his wounds cleaned and dressed, fed the broth from boiling meat and administered to by the medicine man, a gnarled, wrinkled, toothlessly grinning oldster, Julien, in the days that followed, at least continued to hold his own. The leg wound, and the wound in his arm began slowly to heal. But the chest wound, which festered and ran, still gaped open and raw and red.

Yet something sustained the life in this man. Perhaps it was sheer will, which would not let him die. Or perhaps it was something else—a need that even he could not comprehend.

Each day, the medicine man would shake his head as he left. Each day he would mutter to himself that this one could not long continue to live. And yet, Julien Tremeau hung on.

His father came to see him often, marveling with a kind of wondering awe that his son still breathed. It was eerie. No man could go on with a hole like that in his chest.

Night Star, kneeling beside Julien where he lay on a pile of buffalo robes, watched his face with dumb, worshiping eyes. She saw each twist it made with pain, saw, too, the expressions it held as, for a while, his mind wandered in the past.

Never did she leave for more than a few minutes at a time.

31

And never did she doubt. Julien belonged to her. And Julien would live.

Ground mescal buttons, sprinkled into the wound and fed to him by mouth, reduced the pain. Maggots, deliberately put into the wound by the medicine man, devoured the dead and decaying flesh. And in a twilight of half death, half life, Julien Tremeau breathed harshly with what seemed like angry determination.

Weeks passed, and months. Raiding parties of angry and incensed braves roamed the land. Not an isolated ranch remained unburned. Scarcely a stagecoach or a wagon traveled the roads between Denver and the East without suffering attack.

Nor was this the worst. Winter still lay upon the land. The horse herds of the Indians were thin and poor. When new grass came, the war would begin in earnest.

Julien knew none of this. He was like a man hanging on a precipice by the tenuous grip of one hand. Yet the strength of his grip was almost frightening, at least to Charles Tremeau, who muttered one cold morning in January: "I wish he'd let go. I almost wish to God he'd die. There's somethin' wrong about the way he's hangin' on. It's as though that nigger's got somethin' to do, somethin' he's got to do before he dies. And I'm afraid I know just what that somethin' is."

Not hearing, not feeling, unknowing, Julien dreamed, or vaguely remembered the years that had gone before.

He had found Charles and his mother in the Cheyenne village on the banks of Bijou Creek. It was a large village of nearly three hundred lodges. And busy. They had located a herd of buffalo, and each morning the braves went out and each evening returned, their ponies loaded with meat and hides.

Squaws and girls worked in every available space, stretching or fleshing hides, scraping and cleaning entrails, stripping and drying meat. A gray cloud of flies hung over the village, and several packs of wolves prowled its edges at night.

The air was rich with the smell of cooking meat. And there was a look of contented plenty on the face of every person living in it.

Unrecognized, Julien raised his hand as he rode in, palm forward. In Cheyenne, coming easily to his tongue, he said: "I am the son of Charles Tremeau and of Red Earth Woman. Where can they be found?"

A young woman stepped forward to answer him, then flushed prettily and lowered her glance when she had done so. Julien studied her, feeling something stir within him as he did. This one was as unlike the girls he had known as night from day. Strong, lithe, her skin like soft brown velvet. . . .

He found the teepee of Charles Tremeau, entered, and said: "I am Julien, Father, and I am home to stay."

Days of riding to the hunt, his skin bare to the sun and wind, his hair whipping out behind his head. Days of excitement, and friendship with those he had known as a boy. Days of straining competition to excel, to earn his place. And nights—nights when he played the lute before the teepee of Cut Nose, whose daughters were Bird Woman and the young Night Star.

Sometimes the blood beat intolerably hot in his veins as Bird Woman came to talk with him. It was surprising that he, who had shown little restraint with the girls in St. Louis, could now restrain himself. But respect for Cheyenne custom was a deeply inherent part of him.

There was never much doubt that he would take this girl as his wife—never doubt in Julien's mind—never doubt in the girl's. Charles, somewhat reluctantly, gathered a herd of horses and other gifts to be given to Cut Nose, since Bird Woman had no brothers. There was feasting and waiting, while a teepee was prepared for the couple.

33

And now, at last, on his pallet in the teepee of Gray Wolf, Julien Tremeau groaned and stirred. His face was hot with the memory of her—her softness, her warmth, her eager strength that first sweet night. . . .

He opened his eyes, and they fell on the face of Night Star beside him.

Her eyes brimmed with sudden tears.

Julien smiled weakly. "Night Star. Where is Bird Woman? And the children?"

Her tears rolled across her smooth cheeks and dropped unheeded to her lap.

Julien's eyes grew hard, demanding. "Where?"

"Bird Woman is dead."

He flinched visibly. For an instant his eyes lost their hardness, but only for an instant. "The children? Where are they?"

Night Star looked at her hands. "I do not know. I hid them. And I hid myself, but not so well. Two men found me. I fought. The noise must have frightened the children, because they began to make sounds. I broke away and ran, hoping the men would follow. One of them struck me, and I knew no more. When I became conscious again, they both were gone. The children were also gone. Perhaps the men took them." She shuddered visibly. "Then I began to search for you. I found you where you had fallen, and my sister with you. I covered your body with my own to keep you warm. . . ."

Julien moved, and his face twisted with pain. "The men," he said harshly in English. "What did they call each other? Damn it, I've got to have some place to start."

Night Star frowned. She tried desperately to remember. But she failed.

Julien gripped her arm fiercely. "Think! Damn it, think!"

"Jess. . . ." Her face brightened with relief. "And Jack."

"That's all?"

She nodded. She stared at his face, at its heightened color. She stared at his bright, rational eyes. Something sang in her heart. He would live now, surely. He would mend and get well.

Mend? Indeed he would. Swiftly. Quickly. For there was no more time to spare. With brooding eyes—with eyes as gray as smoke—he stared at the winter sky through the hole at the teepee top. He remembered now.

Attack, coming in the gray of dawn, without warning. Murder, rolling down the slope of the bluff like thunder in a summer sky. Grapeshot ripping through the tough hide coverings of the lodges like stones through thin paper—a woman, clutching her breasts while the blood leaked redly between her fingers—a little girl, stumbling over Julien's own prone body and falling, only to be riddled with bullets where she lay. . . .

He had not seen the worst, and this he knew. He hadn't witnessed the death of his wife. He hadn't seen the deaths of his two children, or those of his friends. Nor had he seen the mutilation he knew must have taken place, nor the looting, nor the gleaming eyes and taut, lusting expressions of the soldiers, wallowing in their bath of blood.

"How many?" he croaked. "How many in all?"

His father, stepping through the teepee flap, supplied the answer to that. "Couple hundred at least . . . killed. Couple . . . three hundred more wounded. Mebbe half of them died before they could get to help."

"Where were you?"

"Bent's Fort the night before. I tried to get to you in time. But they'd thrown a guard around the stockade. I got out, but I didn't have a horse. Time I got to the village, it was too damned late."

"Black Feather and Little Bird . . . what about them? Do you think they're dead?"

Charles Tremeau shrugged, watching his son with speculative

eyes. "I didn't find 'em, and I searched that village from one end to the other. Them kids couldn't've gotten very far. . . ."

Blood of his blood, fruit of his own body, borne from the womb of Bird Woman, that slender, brown-skinned girl, now dead. Julien said dully: "Maybe the wolves . . . ?"

His father shrugged. "Maybe." His eyes still rested on Julien's face. "Now what?"

"You have to ask me that?"

"You ain't well yet, hoss."

"I'm well enough."

"For what?"

"For what I've got to do."

He would say no more than that. He raised himself to an elbow, wincing, grimacing with the pain of it. His face turned pale and beaded with sudden sweat. He looked at his wasted body, so white now, so weak. It was like a skeleton compared to the body he had known. He said: "How long? My God, how long has it been?"

"Couple months. Maybe a little more."

Julian looked at Night Star. "Bring me food."

She brought it, and spooned it into his mouth, for he was still too weak to do it for himself. And yet, as she fed him and watched the implacable expression that stayed in his eyes, her heart leaped with fierce joy. There was now no longer any doubt. Julian Tremeau would live. If the children also lived, he would find them. If they did not. . . . Her eyes were suddenly vulnerable. She would give him more to take their places.

Weak from exertion, he fell back and went to sleep. But in a couple of hours he wakened again, and demanded food for the second time that day.

And so it went. Sleeping, eating, sleeping again, he gradually began to put on weight. The wound in his chest began to close in on itself from the edges. Eventually it ceased to drain and closed altogether, although it left a depression in his right breast large enough to enclose Night Star's clenched and trembling hand.

Came the day, at last, in late February, when he left his bed, dressed with Night Star's help, and tottered to the door. Out he went, into the thin sunlight, the raw air, and looked at the sky, at the rolling plain, at the people of the village as they went about their daily tasks. He saw the horse herd, grazing on the south slope of a hill, loosely held by half a dozen boys. He saw an eagle wheeling high overhead. He looked toward the south and west, and remembered that day again, remembered the horror that had come thundering out of the dawn.

His eyes were cold. Soon he would be well. And then the white men would discover what horror really was. But first there was another thing to do.

Night Star stood at his elbow, gazing at his face with worried eyes. He said harshly: "Get me a horse. And provisions. It is time to go."

She hesitated, but did not protest. Her eyes stricken, she turned submissively away.

Julian walked through the village until he found the teepee of his father, Charles Tremeau. He entered, brushed aside his father's pleased exclamation, and said: "Cut my hair. Give me white men's clothes. I am leaving now."

Charles started to protest. His protest died in his throat. He looked at Julien's eyes and looked away. He said gruffly: "All right, hoss. Sit down here, whilst I get my shears."

He came back and began to cut Julien's hair. When he had finished, he dug in his possibles sack until he came up with an outfit of white men's clothes, including a heavy Mackinaw and wide-brimmed hat. He tossed them to Julien, saying as he did: "Been a rumor around for about a week. Don't know if they's anything to it or not."

"What kind of a rumor?" Julien's eyes were cold.

"About some kids . . . two, three, I've heard it both ways . . . on exhibit in a carnival show over at Denver."

Julien nodded. "I'll look into it."

He started to go, but Charles stopped him at the entrance flap. "Lot o' hate in you, Son. Too much. Don't let it eat you up."

Julien didn't reply. He pulled his arm loose from Charles's grasp and went outside.

Hate? His father was right. All the hate in a hating, blood-mad world lay in his heart like a burning core. Bird Woman, that laughing, brown-skinned girl, mother of his children, was decaying in the earth. Never again would she lie, warm and eager, in his arms at night. Never again would she swell with his child, or hold one at her breast. His throat closed until he could scarcely breathe. His eyes burned and his chest felt tight.

Deliberately, angrily he put her from his mind. He thought, instead, of those cannon on the ridge, of the sound they made as they bellowed out their dirge of death. He remembered the squaw, clutching her bleeding breasts, and the child, the girl, riddled a few feet from Julien himself. Most of all, he made himself remember the expressions that had been on the faces of the soldiers as they streamed down the side of the bluff.

Hate? Never had he seen hatred more concentrated than he had that day. But then he had not seen his own face, either. Not for a long, long time.

Night Star brought his horse and sacks of food, which she tied on the horse. Charles Tremeau and Red Earth Woman, aging and ailing, came to see him off. He mounted and would have ridden away, but his father stopped him and handed up a heavy buckskin sack. "I ain't sure I like what you're doin', boy. I ain't sure I like what I figger is in your mind. But where you're goin', you're sure as hell goin' to need a lot of this."

Julien nodded and took the sack. The slightest softening touched his eyes and mouth. He looked down at Night Star. Her eyes held the same expression he had so often seen in the eyes of Bird Woman. The resemblance wrenched his heart.

He turned, and rode away to the northwest, scowling, his gray eyes hard as bits of slate. And he did not look back.

V

All the rest of the day he rode, though he could feel strength fading with each mile the horse traveled. He rode carefully, for he was dressed as a white man now, and after Sand Creek it was unlikely that any white man was safe alone out here.

It was possible that, if discovered, he could make his identity known in time. It was also possible that he could not. So he rode with care, using every trick known to the prairie tribes for traveling unobserved.

That night, he camped in a dry arroyo and ate cold pemmican, a mixture of tallow and dried meat, with chokecherries added to give it flavor and tang. He drank cold water from the narrow stream in the bottom of the draw. He picketed his horse so that the animal could graze. Then he slept like the dead, until the morning sun beat directly into his eyes.

He was stronger than yesterday, if a bit more tired. He mounted and rode again. Today, he could see the thin blue line that hung just above the western horizon. These were the mountains, at the foot of which the town of Denver lay. Denver. The end of his search perhaps. Or the beginning. Only time could tell.

He had little real hope that the children were alive. He had little hope that the rumor was even true. Not that some white men were not capable of exhibiting Indian children in a cage like prairie animals. But there were others. There were decent whites, to whom such a thing would be intolerable. Or so he thought—in spite of Sand Creek, in spite of the things his own two eyes had seen.

The second night it snowed, and he shivered in another draw, much like the first, throughout the night. Again without a fire. For he did not wish to die at the hands of his own good friends.

The third day, a little before noon, he rode down a snowy hill and saw the burgeoning town of Denver lying at its foot.

Manned cannon gaped at him as he rode in. A roughly dressed civilian called to him to halt. "Just a minute, there, bucko. How come you're sashayin' around the prairie all by yourself? And how come you still got all your hair?"

Julien looked at him. Had this one been at Sand Creek? Was this one of those who had streamed toward him down that hill?

The man raised his rifle. He cocked the hammer. He swallowed as though his mouth was dry.

Julien smiled, a cold smile that did not extend to his eyes. He said: "I'm a careful man."

The other eyed his horse, eyed the Indian trappings.

"Where'd you get that hoss?" he asked suspiciously.

"From an Indian," said Julien. "The Indian's dead."

The other man relaxed. "All right. Go on in."

The man was a fool, thought Julien as he rode away. A stupid, gullible fool. But his knees were trembling and he knew it had been close.

He entered the town, and rode down the snowy streets, sliding in the mud underneath the snow. His horse laid back his ears, and rolled his eyes at the buildings, at the people, particularly at the women.

Julien went to the Elephant Corral, stabled his horse, and took a room.

An air of fear was in the town, evidenced by the cannon and armed men guarding the approaches to it, evidenced by the fact that no one went unarmed.

Julien found a saloon in a one-room log cabin not far from the Elephant Corral, and ordered himself a drink. He drank it swiftly and followed it, as swiftly, with another. Taste of the raw whiskey brought him memories of his earlier life in St. Louis. He brushed them impatiently away.

The bartender was watching him strangely. Glancing into the mirror, Julien could understand why. Night Star had kept his face clean-shaven all the time she had cared for him. Now it was covered with a three-day growth. And it was hollow, haunted, like the face of death. Eyes sunk deep in cadaverous sockets, cheeks hollow and gaunt, a mouth thin-lipped and cruel, and angry, too.

His clothes hung like sacks on his bony frame. His wrists stuck out of his sleeves like sticks, seeming too frail to support the weight of his large and bony hands.

He forced a grin. "Hear there's a carnival in town. I been sick a spell. I could do with a little excitement."

The bartender seemed visibly relieved. "There's a carnival, mister, such as it is. Mostly it's just a museum of Injun stuff."

Julien felt tight inside. "Any Indians?"

He waited, clenching his fists at his sides. He realized that he had broken into a sweat, that his knees had begun to shake. Weakness. And damn it, there wasn't time for weakness.

The man said: "Was. Three Injun kids. I ain't been around except that first time, so I don't know if they're still alive or not. One of 'em was coughin' when I was there. Looked pretty sick."

"Where is this place? And when was it you were there?"

"Couple weeks ago. It's over acrost on the other side of the creek, a block up from here. Can't miss it. There's a big sign. . . ."

But Julien was gone.

He hated the man because, though he had not approved the display of Indian children in cages like animals, he had not

41

protested. But as he hurried along, other emotions twisted his thoughts. He remembered the two children, Black Feather and Little Bird. When last he'd seen them, on the morning of the attack, they'd been sleeping peacefully, fat and happy, on either side of Night Star.

That would be changed. He was prepared for that. They would have learned the meaning of fear and, however young and small they were, of hate. They would be thin and dirty, and their eyes would be older than their years.

He crossed the McGaa street bridge, and saw the sign, red against a black background: *Wild West Carnival.* And beneath that: *Jack Ludens, Prop.*

It was a tent, a big one, probably one left over from the town's first days. Probably it had been used as a saloon tent. Snow on its top made the dirty canvas sag. Nothing stirred around it.

His breath made a cloud in the frosty air. He stepped inside the tent. Just as cold inside as it was outside. And a dreary place. A line of cages along one side containing a wolf, a coyote, a bobcat. Some smaller boxes with glass tops containing sluggish, sleeping rattlesnakes. Indian weapons and an assortment of guns hanging against a false wall made of rough-sawed pine. A cluster of dried scalps. And another, larger cage far at the back of the tent.

Julien looked around, his eyes searching for movement. He saw none. His nostrils pinched involuntarily against the smell of the place. Offal from the animals, and maybe from the children, too. Spilled whiskey. Stale tobacco smoke. The sawdust underfoot.

Julien's hands were trembling. Something jerked violently in his stomach. He wanted to lunge across the tent and rip at the bars of the cages. Yet now, fear struck suddenly at his heart.

Slowly, a reluctant step at a time, he crossed the tent. Were the children still there? Were they indeed his two?

The cage, which was about five feet square, was covered in front with iron bars two inches apart. There was a door at one end, with a padlock hasp on it and an unlocked padlock hanging in the hasp.

Julien reached the cage, which appeared empty save for a pile of ragged, filthy blankets in one corner. There was a pan of water on the floor, but it was frozen hard.

He lunged around the end and yanked open the door. He stepped inside, stooping. He seized one of the blankets and yanked it back. The cage was empty. There was nothing here. Nothing but the smell of living things given no opportunity to be clean, of hopelessness and terror worse than death.

They were dead. All three. And why not? Terror alone could have killed them, without the help of the bitter cold, poor rations, sickness.

Julien turned and stepped out. He walked along the line of cages toward the entrance. A wolf bared its teeth at him. The bobcat crouched and snarled.

While yet twenty feet from the door, he saw a man step through. The man saw him and said angrily: "Hey, god damn it, I ain't in this business fer nothin'. Admission's a quarter."

Julien looked at him and the man took an involuntary backward step. Julien wanted the man's dirty neck between his hands. He wanted him spread-eagled on the ground, so that he could make him suffer the way those children must have suffered.

But not quite yet. First he had to know. If the children were still alive, he had to know where they were.

"Where are those Indian children?"

"Ain't got 'em no more. Now gimme my quarter an' get out of here. I ain't even opened the place yet."

Julien stepped close, and his voice was very soft. "Where are they?"

43

The man swallowed, scowled belligerently, then swallowed again. "Hell, it ain't no god-damn' secret. They took 'em away from me. Made me put a price on 'em, then paid it an' took 'em away."

Julien seized the man by the collar of his coat. In spite of his thinness, there was the strength of steel in his hands. "Who? Damn you to hell, who?"

"Fella named Jennings. Some high muck-a-muck in the gov'mint he said."

The man's face was close to his own, the reek of his breath in Julien's nostrils. This one had been at the camp at Sand Creek. This one had. . . .

The need to kill was sudden and overpowering. The man began to struggle. "Get out of here, damn it. You got no right to come bustin' in here like this. Who'n hell are you, anyhow?"

Julien could leave him here, dead and broken on the sawdust floor. He could slip a knife between his ribs before. . . . But it wouldn't be enough. And he wouldn't take the chance. Later, there would be time for vengeance. Now he had to find the children.

He flung the man from him. Ludens tripped and almost fell. His hand started toward the gun at his side. Julien only looked at him. If Ludens's hand touched that gun, before he could get it clear Julien's knife would be buried in his chest.

Ludens changed his mind. He glared at Julien with sullen defiance until Julien stalked outside.

Three children, caged like animals, sold like slaves. It didn't matter that Jennings, whoever he was, had acted because the barbarity of the childrens' captivity had sickened even the government. The hard, cold facts were that the government had recognized Ludens's right to his captives by paying his price for them. Nor had they punished him.

But Julien would. Black Dog would. After he had found the

children and rescued them.

Jennings. Representing the government. But what government? United States? Territorial? Or the town government? He didn't know.

He wandered toward the bridge, scowling. A lightness was in his head, an odd feeling he had never known before. And combined with it was another feeling—almost a certainty. He would never find the children because they no longer were alive.

Ransomed because their presence in those cages was an abomination decent people could not stand. But ransomed too late. They could not have lived long under those conditions, in that icy tent. They could not have remained healthly, half naked, half starved, without hope and frightened almost to death.

He realized he was running and breathing hard. He hauled up and leaned, panting, against a building wall. The streets were crowded now. Passersby stared at him, some with curiosity, some with apprehension.

The light feeling remained in his brain. He looked at those that stared, hating each one individually, as he had never hated anything before in his life. They did not belong here. They were interlopers, despoilers of a good, rich land that belonged to the prairie tribes. They were murderers—and worse.

His eye caught a sign: *Rocky Mountain News*. What better place to get the information he had to have than this?

Staggering from weakness and the intensity of his own emotions, he crossed the street and went inside. He fought for composure. He'd get nothing, no information, no help, unless he controlled himself.

His voice was calm as he spoke, but calm with a visible effort to make it so. "I'm a stranger. But I understand there were three Indian children on exhibit in that carnival tent down the street. Can you tell me what happened to them?"

The man facing him was shorter than he, a gentle-faced man

with a trimmed brown beard and mustache. He frowned. "Shameful. A disgrace to our city."

Julien clenched his fists. His voice held an awful intensity that made the man glance at him uneasily. "What happened to them?"

"They're dead, I'm afraid. A representative of the government . . . the Colorado Territorial government . . . ransomed them two weeks ago. They were ill, all three of them. Looked like consumption to me. They were taken to Doctor Hargrave, but, as I say, it was too late."

"Where can I find Doctor Hargrave?"

The newspaperman studied him critically, then shook his head. "It occurred to me that you might be an Eastern newspaperman, but I guess you're not. All right. Doctor Hargrave's place is on F Street, over the Cooper Saddlery."

Julien nodded. He went outside. They were dead, then. All three of them. Dead—of cold, hunger, neglect, fear. Dead because of the apathy or outright cruelty of those who paid a quarter to see them but would raise no hand to help. Dead because of Jack Ludens and the unknown man called Jess.

As though in a daze, Julien wandered along the street. Twice, he stopped someone to ask directions.

How would he know—indeed would he ever know—if those child captives had included his own beloved two?

He found Dr. Hargrave's place. The doctor, an old, tired, bearded man, lived alone over the saddlery shop and maintained a four-bed ward as a kind of hospital. Almost dazedly he talked to the man.

"Yes, sir, Mister, uh . . . ?"

"Tremeau."

"Mister Tremeau. I got 'em a couple of weeks ago from a Mister Jennings. All three of 'em had consumption. Damn' little I could do. I cleaned 'em up, put 'em to bed, and did everything

I could. They all died in less than a week. Poor little things."

"Where are they buried?"

"Down by the river. Paid for that out of my own pocket."

"Who buried them?" Julien seized him by the shoulders. His eyes burned into the doctor's. "Who?"

"Connors's helper downstairs." The doctor watched him, without fear, but with tired concern. "You're sick yourself."

Julien corrected: "I was sick."

He went out, down the outside stairway.

There was an old man dumping trash behind the shop. Julien walked around the building. "You Connors's helper?"

"Uhn-huh. Dooley's the name."

"Where'd you bury those three Indian children?"

"Down by the river. Why?"

"Show me."

The man hesitated. Julien fished a gold eagle from his pocket. The man looked at him suspiciously. "That's four times what I got fer buryin' 'em."

"Damn you, take me to the place. Bring a shovel."

The man tried to pull away. His eyes were suddenly frantic with fear. Julien said flatly: "Run, or yell, and I'll put this knife between your shoulder blades."

"All right. All right! I'll take you."

Julien followed him as he scurried down the alley, thence toward the river. They left the town behind. Fifteen minutes later, the man halted.

Julien said: "Dig!" His face twisted. His fists clenched tightly.

The man began to dig, trembling so violently he could scarcely work. "You ain't goin' to kill me, are you?"

"I don't know. Dig."

The terrified man whined: "They ain't very deep, but it ain't my fault. This frozen ground . . . I'm an old man. . . ."

"Dig, damn you."

The old man dug. After a while, at a depth of less than a foot, he stopped. "Here they are." He was watching Julien's face, his own face twisted with fear at what he saw there.

The old man shambled away. Twice he fell, slipping on the snowy ground in his almost frantic haste. Julien watched coldly until he was out of sight.

Then he knelt in the shallow grave. With very gentle, trembling hands, he pushed aside the clods of frozen earth until he had uncovered one small face—another—the third.

Suddenly his shoulders shook. Tears streamed down his bearded cheeks and dripped unheeded into the small, white, upturned faces.

How long he stayed thus he could not have said. But at last he straightened and gently took the bodies, one by one, from the grave. He laid them side-by-side on the snowy ground, laid his Mackinaw over them. Then he walked toward town to get his horse.

Black Feather—and Little Bird—and another, who he did not know. They must be buried again—but deeply and reverently, and with his own two hands—out on the wide, vast plain where they belonged.

Then, and only then, would he return.

VI

From the hard-packed floor, where Julien had flung him, Jack Ludens watched him leave. He had never experienced anything quite like this before, but his body had suddenly become like ice. His stomach felt empty, hollow. And even though the stranger was gone, it seemed to Ludens as though he were still looking at the man, so strongly was the memory of his appearance etched upon Ludens's brain.

Those sunken, burning eyes. . . . He shivered in spite of himself. And that thin-lipped mouth, the hollow cheeks, the high-domed forehead whose skin was tightly stretched and like parchment, almost, in its texture. He would see that face in his sleep—he would see it in all his waking hours.

He knew something else. Not only in his thoughts would he see that face. He would see it again, in reality, a few seconds before he died. He wished, suddenly, that he'd never heard of Chivington's Volunteers. He wished he'd never enlisted, that he'd never seen the Cheyenne village on Sand Creek, that he'd never taken those damned kids.

Too late for wishing. He had taken the children, and now they all were dead. What the stranger's connection with them was, he had no idea. Perhaps the man was simply incensed over what had happened to them. Yet Ludens felt instinctively that it was more than that. The stranger's concern was personal. And when he found that they all had died, he would be coming back.

Ludens got up almost frantically. He hadn't much time. It was only a matter of hours, maybe minutes, until the stranger would be directed to Doc Hargrave's place. That damned Byers had run an indignant article about the children the day after Jennings had taken them. He'd mentioned the doctor's name.

Ludens shook his head. He would never understand people. Six months ago the whole town was talking about exterminating every damned Indian on the plains, as if they were some kind of varmints. So why all this sudden concern about a few Indian pups that died? Hell, Ludens hadn't killed them. God, no. He'd saved their lives, as a matter of fact. If it hadn't been for him, Jess Durand would have dashed out their brains against that Indian hearth.

People got sick all the time. It happened, damn it. Just because those Indian children died. . . . He realized that his thoughts were becoming frantic. He ran to the door. He looked up the street and saw the stranger, running, half a block away.

There was a lithe, smooth way about the stranger's run, but it was also unsteady, as though from weakness, or drink.

Ludens looked back at the interior of his tent. Everything he had was here, little as it was. And until the business of those damned kids getting sick, it had paid him a fair living. He couldn't leave it just because some stranger came in asking about the kids.

But the stranger's face hung like a cloud in his thoughts. And his body felt cold. The thing to do, he decided, was to follow the stranger and find out what he was up to, what he wanted. Maybe Ludens wouldn't have to run. Maybe his fear was only imagination.

He stepped out of the tent and, at a fast walk, went up the street. The stranger wasn't hard to keep in sight. He kept stopping, and at last he halted and leaned against a building wall, directly across from the *Rocky Mountain News*.

Ludens halted, too, half a block away. He watched the stranger cross the street and go into the office of the *Rocky Mountain News*. Later he saw him come out again and turn uptown. At intervals, the stranger stopped someone, spoke a few words, and then went on. Ludens gathered that he was asking directions, for those he talked to usually pointed.

Eventually the stranger reached the Cooper Saddlery on F Street and climbed the outside stairs to Hargrave's office. He was gone only a little while, and then returned. He went out behind the saddle shop and talked to an old man dumping trash. The two went off together. It was plain, even from where Ludens watched, that the old man was scared.

Ludens had seen enough. The stranger was personally concerned in this. He'd tracked down those kids like a hunting dog. First the *Rocky Mountain News*, where he'd been directed to Doc. Then to the handyman downstairs, who logically would have been the one Doc got to bury them. Then off to the site of the grave with a shovel.

Ludens was almost running as he turned away and headed for his tent. Only briefly did he consider going after the stranger and killing him. It wouldn't work. There was something about the man—something eerie. And even if Ludens succeeded in killing him—well, things had changed in Denver lately. You couldn't just up and kill someone and get away with it. There'd been some hangings of men who had thought they could.

The thing to do was to run, get out of town, go where that icy, murderous stranger would never find him. To hell with the tent. He could get another. And next time. . . .

Out of breath, he stopped. He forced himself to walk along at a pace that would attract neither notice nor comment. He reached the tent and threw a few things he'd need into a possibles sack. He went out back to get his horse.

How much time did he have? An hour? Two? Or would the stranger wait until tomorrow to come after him? He didn't know. What he did know was that he wasn't going to waste a minute more. If he got out now, that stranger would never pick up his trail. This was too big a town. You couldn't circle it and check every trail that left.

He rode away from his tent without looking back. He might have salvaged something, either by trying to sell the thing, or by getting someone to run it for him. But that would have left a trail.

He reached the upper end of town, saw the guards, and turned back. Even this would leave a trail. No, he would have to slip out, somehow, at an unguarded spot on the town's rim.

He thought of the empty miles of prairie out there, thought of the stories he'd heard and read of Indian atrocities since the Sand Creek affair. He shivered slightly and looked back toward the heart of town, his decision to leave wavering. Then he remembered the stranger. He saw that face again in his thoughts.

He had to have time to think. He had to plan a course. Running off like this, acting like a panic-stricken rabbit was the stupidest thing he could do. But his time was running out. Aimlessly, fearfully he rode the streets. There was no safety here. Nor was there safety on the plains.

Eventually he stabled his horse on the west side of the creek. He took a room for the night in one of the less savory of the rooming houses there, and closed and locked the door.

He couldn't have gone far tonight anyway, he assured himself. Not far enough, if that man was after him.

He tried to sleep, and couldn't. Eventually he went down to the bar and bought a bottle of cheap whiskey. But the liquor produced no artificial glow of well-being as it usually did. It didn't even make him sleep. Instead, it seemed to turn his fears into grotesque things, as unreal as the monstrosities of a nightmare. And so he spent the night, bathed with sweat, yet cold, all but unconscious and yet awake. When morning finally came, a pale gray line over the eastern plain, he was glad to go, glad to face the plain or even a horde of vengeful Cheyennes. Anything was better than the face he saw in his thoughts, and the terror that was beginning to grow in his heart.

He slipped out of town unseen by leading his horse down the bed of Cherry Creek in the first cold gray of dawn. At the junction of the creek with the Platte, he turned south. The nearest safety lay at Bent's Fort on the Arkansas. Perhaps there would be a caravan going East. Or perhaps he could travel to Independence with an Army supply train from Fort Lyon nearby.

Anything was better than the regularly traveled stage routes along the Platte and Smoky Hill River. Hardly a coach arrived these days that had not been attacked. Many simply did not arrive.

He rode until the sun came up, then stopped to build a small fire in a shallow gulch. He boiled some water and made coffee. His head was splitting from the whiskey he'd consumed. The coffee made his stomach knot with nausea. The wind was bitterly cold, blowing down off the snow-buried peaks of the Continental Divide. The sun gave little warmth. He killed his fire, mounted again, and went his haunted way.

All morning he rode, and well into the afternoon, before he began to feel a lessening of his fear. He was damned near halfway to Bent's Fort by now. That stranger would never catch him. It might take the man a week to figure out his trail. He might never figure it out. In fact, the stranger might not even look for a trail, and instead assume that Ludens had hidden himself in town.

In addition, Ludens's hangover was wearing itself out. He was hungry now, and even began to look forward to arriving in the East again. He began to plan another carnival. An Indian museum. That ought to go over real big back East. People there were intensely interested in life out here on the plains. Planning thus, he rode faster, but as watchfully as before.

The sun sank out of sight in the west. The shades of dusk deepened into night. Ludens had intended to ride all night, but the sleeplessness of last night was now beginning to tell on him. He looked around for a place to camp, wishing he'd used more forethought when he had left town. The only provisions he had were a sack of beans and a little coffee.

He topped a low rise and suddenly, before him and about a mile away, he saw the winking light of a fire. He halted abruptly, a small chill touching his spine. He looked around at the darkness, imagining Indians surrounding him. He heard nothing, and nothing moved. Had he been wiser in the ways of the plains, he would have known that in these times only a man who did not fear the Indians would dare build a fire at night.

But Ludens did not know this, or think of it, and so his courage began to return. It was doubtful, he realized, if an Indian would dare build a fire here on the direct route between Denver and Fort Lyon. It was doubtful if a single Indian would dare show himself so plainly here at night.

Nor was it likely that a fire that small could belong to more than one man. It couldn't belong to a party of braves strong enough to risk building it.

Reassured, he approached the fire cautiously. It winked in the night like a small yellow star, a friendly fire that promised warmth and food and, most of all, companionship against the terror of the night and the face that haunted his thoughts.

A couple of hundred yards away, he halted again and tied his horse to a clump of brush. He approached cautiously on foot. All he could see in the fire's light was the back of a lone man, sitting beside it and staring into it. The man was obviously white.

Silently Ludens walked in. Relief made him feel loose and relaxed. He could sleep tonight. He could sleep, and by tomorrow that face would be nothing more than a fading memory.

Something vague and obscure still bothered him. He chuckled nervously to himself. He was probably imagining danger. He had probably exaggerated the menace he'd thought he'd felt in that stranger. He might have been feeling a little guilty about those kids. Perhaps somewhere in the back of his mind he hadn't felt quite right about imprisoning human beings as though they were some kind of prairie varmint. He called out: "Howdy, friend! Got room at that fire fer . . . ?"

His voice froze in his throat, which seemed to constrict until he couldn't breathe. He shook his head and blinked his eyes. The vague something that had troubled him was now plain enough. He'd seen those clothes before.

But it couldn't be! Out of a dozen possible directions, he had come this one. A dozen, a hundred, a thousand to one were the odds against this being true.

But it was true, and the face of the man turning toward him was the face that had haunted his thoughts. He was staring straight at Julien Tremeau.

Like a moth trapped in a spider's web, he struggled with his heavy coat, trying to get his gun. His fingers were thumbs, his hands like stumps.

Not so with Julien Tremeau. He moved like a cat to the kill. Across the space between the two he came, an expression of fierce, unbelieving joy in his eyes. It was not the God of the white men who had helped him tonight, but Heammawihio, god of the Cheyennes. Heammawihio was on his side, and had made this come to pass. Now he did not need to go back and kill this one. For this one had come to him.

In a flurry of action beyond the rim of the fire's light, Ludens went down before the lighter weight, but almost fanatical strength of Julien Tremeau.

But he did not die. Not yet. To Julien Tremeau, raised in an Indian camp, that would have been too easy. The odd, light feeling in Julien's head was growing now and he knew it would never go away. Not until all those who had died at Sand Creek had been avenged.

VII

Only the night heard Ludens's screams, and only the night witnessed the vengeance that Julien Tremeau wreaked on him.

It was Black Dog, the Cheyenne Indian, who stripped Ludens and staked him out on the frozen ground. It was Black Dog who, when he tired of the screams, cut out Ludens's tongue. Black Dog the Cheyenne built a fire on Ludens's belly and coldly watched it burn.

But it was Julien Tremeau who, staring down with pale face and burning eyes said: "Two of those children were mine."

Then mercifully buried his knife in Ludens's heart. And, before turning away, it was Julien Tremeau who scratched the initials *JT* on the ground beside the naked and mutilated body. And after it the numeral *1*.

Let them know who had killed this man. Their eyes would tell them how. Let them know, too, that Ludens was only the first. There would be many, many more.

What is the price, in human lives, of the lives of your son and daughter? What is the price of their suffering, before they were able to die?

This was only a part of that price, and even with this paid there were other scores to be settled. For Bird Woman, brown-skinned, laughing. For the others, the innocent ones who had been mutilated just as Ludens had.

The old lightness was in Julien's head as he mounted his horse and headed east through the starry night, lightness but partially relieved by the small vengeance he had achieved.

Behind him, Ludens stared at the night sky with blank and sightless eyes. Wolves, drawn by the smell of blood, warily circled the embers of the dying fire.

Jake Bauer found him in the morning, drawn to the spot by the circling vultures. He watched them rise into the air, flapping, shedding feathers, and repressed a shudder as he always must when he saw them too closely.

He got down from his horse, knowing instantly which of Ludens's wounds had been made by wolves and vultures, which had been made by his killer while he was yet alive.

Two things made Jake frown. The knife wound in Ludens's chest, obviously a fatal one, and the initials and numeral 1, scratched in the ground beside him.

He wrapped the body in a piece of canvas and lashed it down on his pack horse. As he continued on his way, he frowned over those initials. No Indian scratched his initials beside the bodies of his victims. Yet the manner of Ludens's death unmistakably pointed to an Indian as his killer.

Suddenly Bauer's eyes brightened. He scratched his beard and spit chewing tobacco beside his horse. Half-Indian, half-white—a half-breed turned renegade. It was the only answer. It explained the merciful knife in the heart. It explained the initials on the ground.

Who did he know with the initials JT? Who, with a surname beginning with a T? Charles Tremeau. Hank Teeters. He could only think of two.

Tremeau. Tremeau. He frowned. That one had a son—a son half-white, half-red, married to a Cheyenne woman. But that son had been killed at Sand Creek. The sons of Charley Autobeas had seen him lying dead.

Or had they? Wasn't it possible that Julien Tremeau still lived?

A thing for the military in Denver to figure out. It was their problem. One thing alone was sure. If Julien Tremeau still lived, if it was he, indeed, who had done this thing, then the settlers in Colorado Territory had better prepare for war.

The Indians were bad enough. But angry, outraged Indians directed with the cunning of a white. . . . In spite of himself, Jake Bauer could not repress a small, cold shiver of dread.

Thirty miles to the east, Julien Tremeau rode alone, leading the horse Ludens had been riding. His mind was busy with his plans.

The plains held several tribes, Cheyennes, Sioux, Arapahoes, Pawnees, Comanches. Some were friendly with each other. Some were not. But theirs was a loose organization, composed of a vague federation of individual villages, each governed by its own chief, whose edicts were enforced by a core of proven warriors, known as Dog Soldiers.

Never had the tribes wholly united in anything. Never, indeed, had even one tribe acted in concert, without dissenters. But if, by some miracle of diplomacy, the tribes could now unite. . . . Julian's heart soared. Combined, they could put ten to fifteen thousand warriors in the field. Mounted, armed, they could erase the whites from the face of the land. Led by a white, they could put aside their reluctance to fight at night—and the whites wouldn't have a chance.

What better, more glorious vengeance than this? Julien knew there could be no better revenge than what he planned. And while he also knew that the tide of white settlement was inevitable, he was aware that he could bring it to a grinding halt for a score of years.

With lighter heart than before, he spurred his horse ahead. He swung to the south, for he wanted to view the desolation that was left at the site of the massacre. It would spur him on. Looking at the brooding, snowy plain where he had known so much pure joy, he would renew his determination and refresh his love for Bird Woman, who now was dead. He could tell her, wherever she was in that empty waste, that he had avenged their children's deaths.

He arrived on the second day, near evening. The stench of death was gone from the place now, as were most of the signs of death and destruction. Blackened ruins still showed where the village had been—a piece of unburned teepee covering here, a few charred teepee poles there. Rusted weapons lay half buried, in the snow and mud. A whitened bone that some wolf had left. A broken, weathered bow, an arrowhead—a stain that was darker brown than the ground surrounding it. Little enough to show what had taken place. Little enough to remember. Yet he needed no monuments to memory here.

He climbed the bluff, where the troops had massed, from which their cannon had spouted death. He looked at the plain, and at the site of the village below.

How many mornings had he risen and looked at this same wide plain? How many times had he bathed with his children there in that icy stream? How many nights had he lain with Bird Woman in the warmth and safety of his lodge?

His face twisted with pain. His eyes brightened with tears. They all were gone, and nothing now was left. Loneliness beat upon him. He would never see Black Feather grow to be a man. He would have no heirs.

But he would be remembered. His eyes hardened. His mouth twisted. He would be remembered all right. For the thing he had done and the things he would do in the days to come.

Almost regretfully he mounted his horse and turned north toward Smoky Hill. Softness and sentiment were now firmly behind him. He would do what he had to do, and in the end he would die as a man should die.

All through the night he rode without stopping, except to change horses when the one he was riding threatened to give out. He rode most of the morning, too, arriving at the village very near to noon.

He was hungry, and weak, and weary, but, as he dismounted before the lodge, he told Night Star: "Find my father, and find Blue Stone, my friend. Bring them here to me."

He went inside, and nodded to Gray Wolf and his family. He did not even have a lodge of his own, and the lack suddenly made him hate the white men more.

He sat down beside the stone hearth at the center of the lodge and ate the tender dog-meat stew handed to him by Gray Wolf's oldest squaw.

Now that he was back the weakness that he had held back only by the force of will began to overcome him. He struggled against it.

Gray Wolf said: "Black Dog is still sick. He needs to rest."

"There can be no rest for me . . . or for any Cheyenne."

He was interrupted by the entrance of his father, Night Star, and the young Blue Stone. They looked at him expectantly. Night Star brought him new, soft moccasins and began to unlace his heavy leather shoes. Kneeling at his feet, her great, soft eyes never left his face.

Charles Tremeau stared at his son and cleared his throat. "What'd you find out, hoss?" he asked in English.

Julien said in Cheyenne: "I found three children in a grave. Two of them were mine. The other I did not know."

"Oh my God! I'm sorry, boy."

As though speaking to himself, Julien went on, disdaining the use of English. "They were taken at the battle and imprisoned in a dirty, filthy, icy cage, without enough to wear, without enough to eat. The one who had them charged the whites a quarter to come inside and stare at them. Beside their cage were other cages, holding the beasts of the plains. The wildcat. The wolf. And still other cages that held the poisonous prairie snakes."

Charles Tremeau's face mirrored his horror. "No wonder the poor tykes died."

Julien didn't look at him. Almost as though in a daze he continued: "They contracted consumption. At last, even the territorial government was ashamed. Yet even then they did not take them from this man and punish him. They bought my children as though they were slaves and the man their rightful owner. They took them to a doctor who cared for them. But it was now too late. One after another those children died, and were buried by the river in a grave less than a foot deep, side-by-side."

Those in the teepee scarcely breathed. Night Star's eyes welled with tears that spilled over and dripped unheeded from her cheeks. Gray Wolf's face was fierce and angry, as was Blue

Stone's. Charles Tremeau's was soft, with pity and sadness. And in Charles Tremeau another emotion was visible. Fear. Fear of what this had done to his son.

Gray Wolf asked fiercely: "What did you do, Black Dog?"

"I took them from the grave, vowing I would find the one who had captured and caged them and stake him out on the plains. I carried them south on my horse, toward Big Timbers, until I found a peaceful, pretty place that looked across the plains for more than a hundred miles. Here, I buried them deeply, beyond the reach of hungry wolves. And then I prepared to return for my revenge."

Those in the teepee waited now with breathing nearly stilled. Julien was pallid with his memory of that night. He said: "I did not have to return for my revenge. Heammawihio brought the criminal to me. He rode into my camp that night, alone, calling out to me."

No sound marred the utter stillness in the lodge. Julien muttered softly: "He now is dead, his belly blackened by the fire I built upon it, his flesh marked by the edge of my knife."

Expressions of fierce satisfaction, almost of awe, showed on the faces of Gray Wolf and Blue Stone. Not so Charles Tremeau.

Julien looked straight at him, with angry defiance. "On the ground beside his body, I scratched my initials with my knife along with the number one."

His father said: "Then you have made yourself an outlaw."

"So be it. I am not finished yet."

Blue Stone stiffened. "What will you do now?"

Julien looked at him. Blue Stone was younger than he, but a seasoned warrior who had counted many coups, some against the whites. And Blue Stone was his friend, almost fanatically loyal to him for he had saved the younger man's life two years before in a battle with the Shoshones. He said: "Find me ten men who do not wish to accept the abuse the whites have heaped on us. Find me ten men who can hate as I can hate. Then I will tell you what I am going to do."

Blue Stone got up and left. Charles Tremeau studied his son's face. "What are you going to do?"

Julien's eyes blazed. "Unite the tribes of the plains. Teach them that to fight in unison under a single chief is the way to drive the whites forever from their lands."

"You're a white man yourself." Tremeau spoke in English, softly, urgently. "Think, hoss! Don't get carried away. The time will come when here in this very spot there will be farms, and fences, and schools, and maybe even cities. You can't stop them. The tribes, united even, can't stop them."

"Then I will slow them down."

"You'll never unite the tribes. They're too damned independent ever to work together for long."

"Then I will fight alone."

"Why? Why? You can't bring Bird Woman back. You can't bring your children back."

Julien smiled coldly. "I can avenge their deaths."

"You've already done that." Desperation was in Charles Tremeau's voice. He studied his son's face, and an expression of defeat finally touched his eyes. He got to his feet. "Mebbe you'll change your mind. Meantime, me an' your ma got a little surprise for you. Come along."

He held the flap for Julien. Night Star, her face unusually pink, her eyes unusually bright, followed him out.

Charles led him along the village street and stopped at last before a teepee Julien had never seen before. A new one, made, no doubt, since he had been gone.

Tremeau said: "It's yours, hoss. Now go on in and get some rest."

Julien stepped inside. Night Star followed. Charles Tremeau

grinned and returned to his own lodge, and to his own ailing, weakening wife.

He had known much happiness here on the plains, with these people he knew and loved so well. But his heart knew that the old, good days were gone. Each man, who lived as Charles Tremeau had lived, would have to make a choice.

Julien had made his. He would be branded a renegade from one end of the land to the other. Because he was part white, a price would be put upon his head. The bitterest part of it was that Charles's choice could never be the same as his son's. They must go their separate ways.

He told Red Earth Woman none of this. She was dying. This he knew. When she had gone, there would be nothing left to hold him here. He would return to the whites where he belonged.

VIII

Brooding and planning, Julien sat in the center of the teepee, staring into the fire that Night Star had just refreshed. He heard her moving around the lodge with but a small part of his mind. He had no eyes for the flush that stained her cheeks, for the shyness that was in her eyes.

His mind was envisaging a horde of warriors on the plains, sweeping like a tide from one town to the next, burning, pillaging, destroying. Denver must be the first to fall, for it was there that the army of Chivington had grown. Or perhaps they should wait and first take on the smaller towns, to give the warriors experience in fighting as a unit—and to give them arms they did not have.

All of it would have to wait until the spring grass came, until the pony herds fattened and lost their winter hair. For the great strength of the Indian warrior was his mobility. Julien would show them how to strike one place at dawn, strike another half a hundred miles away before dark fell.

Now, while he waited, he needed food and rest. A lot of both. For when the new grass came he must be ready and strong again.

He lay back on the soft profusion of tanned buffalo robes and closed his eyes. Night Star paused to look at him. His mouth had softened with sleep. Still it was strong, but it was no longer cruel. His face had relaxed. Thin and ravaged by his wound, it bore little resemblance to the old Julien Tremeau.

She belonged to him wholly now. And she would make him forget. His thirst for vengeance would fade in a reawakening of his thirst for life. Once more he would know the happy cries of children in his lodge. Once more he would know contentment, and peace.

She told herself these things, and yet could not entirely believe them. Stubbornly she put her unbelieving thoughts away and waited for Black Dog, her man, to waken.

He did, at dusk, and ate hungrily of the stew she had prepared. He went out, then, and bathed in the icy stream. Naked and carrying his white men's clothes, he returned and threw them down, afterward donning the soft, new deerskins she had made for him.

Restlessly he prowled the lodge, prowled the village and the plain beyond. His eyes were fierce, intent. He had forgotten his father, forgotten the young Night Star. He was wholly Indian now.

He began to fight his memories. In plans for war, he put aside the memories of Bird Woman, and Black Feather, and Little Bird. And yet, however he tried, the sight of those three dead faces half covered with frozen clods kept coming back. Memory of the warm, soft nights of summer with Bird Woman in his arms kept recurring in his mind.

He was a tortured man who, though he thought he had made

his choice, had not fully accepted it. A man who had dedicated himself to cruelty and destruction and treachery, but to whom all those qualities were foreign. A man who, even while he tortured the dying Ludens, had, somewhere in the depths of him, felt pity for the man.

Angrily he paced the snowy plain, fighting himself for peace. And at last, near midnight, he returned, exhausted, to his lodge.

It was dark, and the fire was only a bed of dying coals. He laid down and covered himself with robes.

Near him, he could hear the soft, even breathing of Night Star. He closed his eyes. He forced himself to relax.

He dozed, and woke sweating, hearing the cannon booming on the ridge. He dozed again and saw the dead faces of his children in their grave. Then, at last, he felt the warmth, the softness of Bird Woman in his arms.

With a sob he caught her close, nearly crushing her with the fierceness of his hunger and his need. Her tears were wet against his cheeks, her body eager beneath his own. Higher and higher his long-dead passions rose. All thought had ceased, and there was only this. . . .

And then, like a flash of summer lightning, it came to a sudden end. He lay, exhausted and trembling, at her side.

He became aware that this was not a dream. He became slowly aware that this was not Bird Woman at his side.

For an instant, terrible rage burned in the core of his brain. In that brief instant he wanted to kill, to tear apart this woman for thus cheating and deceiving him. He almost yielded to his desire, but caught himself with his hands tightening around her throat.

He got up and burst, half clothed, from the flap of the lodge. He ran silently into the cold, clear night. He plunged himself deliberately into the chilling stream and stayed until he thought he would die of cold.

65

There was an awful need in him that had to be fulfilled. There was hunger, not assuaged by Ludens's death, that could not be denied.

Perhaps he was insane. Perhaps the ordeal at Sand Creek had been too much for him. But he had to kill, and, if he did not kill the hated whites, he might kill the ones he loved.

Charles Tremeau had been right. There was too much hate in him. He must rid himself of it somehow, and he knew of but one sure way. His mind at rest at last, he returned to his teepee and to a terrified Night Star.

Never again would he hesitate; never would he doubt. But even if he did, he would go on and on, until his name was known and feared from one end of the vast plains to the other. He would become the scourge of the plains, the worst desperado the land had ever known.

IX

In the first gray of dawn, Blue Stone came to Julien's lodge with six others. All were mounted, armed, and painted for war. There was Beaver, a man young and quick and anxious to prove himself. There was Iron Horse, older and more seasoned, but as fanatical as Blue Stone himself. There was Rain Cloud, and One-Eye, and Dead Buffalo. Lastly there was Comanche, a young medicine man.

Julien came through the teepee flap and stood looking up at them. He nodded and mounted his horse, which Night Star had earlier gone out and caught for him. He looked down at her, standing in the teepee flap.

There was a resemblance between her and his dead wife that he noticed strongly this morning, perhaps because of the way she looked at him. He turned his head quickly away.

Without looking back, he led the others out of the village and onto the empty plain beyond. He headed north and west.

He had not missed the fact that only he and two others carried firearms. The rest carried lances and bows and quivers of arrows strapped to their backs.

Weapons, then, were their most pressing need. Modern weapons, repeaters if possible. Weapons that were not to be found at isolated ranches or in other Indian camps. Weapons such as those carried by stagecoach drivers and guards. And ammunition in great quantity.

North of Denver by several miles there was a stagecoach way station. This was Julien Tremeau's first objective.

As he rode, silent and cold, he planned. He had eight men, counting himself. Three had rifles, but only his was a repeating rifle capable of more than one shot without reloading. To attack a stagecoach way station with no more than these was to risk heavy losses he could not afford. Heavy losses on this, his first raid, might doom his plan for good. He might be branded bad medicine and be unable to enlist recruits. It must, then, be done in such a way as to hold losses to a minimum. And rewards must be high.

The miles flowed steadily beneath their tireless horses' hoofs. They rode openly and without attempt at concealment.

Steadily northward and westward he led them, and in midafternoon, from a high point a dozen miles east of Denver, they stared at the untidy cluster of buildings, at the rising, distant smoke that was like a thin haze in the air.

His face hardened and his mouth thinned. Again the stench of the cage in the carnival seemed to be in his nostrils. Again that burning hatred seared his mind. And in that instant, he conceived his plan, a treacherous, cruel, and diabolic one, but a plan that would work.

He deliberately slowed his pace. Now he led his braves more carefully for he knew if they were seen the way station he intended to attack might be forewarned.

The cold sun sank slowly toward the mountains in the west. It briefly stained a few thin clouds before it dropped from sight. Gray dusk came quickly to the plain and deepened quickly into night.

A mile east of the way station, Julien drew his horse to a halt atop a knoll. He sat like a stone statue, looking with burning eyes at the dimly twinkling lights.

There was no room in his mind for the thought that down there, clustered about the lights inside the way station, were people of his father's blood. People such as he had known in the East while he was going to school. Good people, innocent of the crime at Sand Creek. There was room in his mind only for hate.

Without speaking, he led his savage followers off the knoll and down toward the lights below, only to halt again three hundred yards away. Speaking in the Cheyenne tongue, he said: "Wait. I will bring them out."

Blue Stone protested: "At night? It is not good to fight at night."

Julien stared at the vague shape nearby. "Blue Stone is afraid to die?"

There was a moment before the answer came, and, when it did, it was touched with both anger and shame. "Blue Stone is not afraid to die. But to die at night is to wander forever alone."

"No one will die tonight. No one save the whites in there. I have a plan." No one answered him. He repeated: "Wait. I will bring them out. When I do, attack immediately. Do you understand?"

Blue Stone's voice held a touch of sullenness. "We understand."

Julien rode closer to the way station. Two hundred yards from it, he dismounted and went on afoot.

Much depended upon his success tonight, so much that he

could feel his hands and legs trembling. He stopped fifty yards short of the door. A coach was in. It was pulled up immediately before the door. Apparently the passengers were inside eating supper, for fresh horses had not yet been hitched to the coach. He could hear movements in the corral behind the way station and occasionally a profane shout.

He lay down behind a clump of brush. He raised his gun and fired a single shot. He waited until a shaft of light from the door bathed the ground, then yelled in a voice that sounded weak and almost incoherent with pain: "Help. For God's sake. . . . I can't. . . ."

He could see them clustered in the doorway. He could see the guns in their hands and could almost feel their suspicion.

He yelled, more weakly now—"Help me. . . ."—and groaned, as though in pain.

He lay still, utterly silent after that. He heard their voices plainly. One man was arguing against going out. The others, apparently in disagreement with him, left the building and crossed the road. The one who had argued against it came along cautiously behind, his gun held ready in his hands. The others had either holstered theirs or left them behind. Two women came through the door and stood in the light, watching curiously.

When the nearest was no more than fifteen feet away, Julien sprang to his feet. He fired with unerring accuracy into the chest of the man with the rifle. He fired again at one of the women and dropped her neatly in the doorway so that the other couldn't close the door. He heard a shrill whoop of triumph and realized it came from his own lips.

An arrow hissed out of the darkness and buried itself with an audible sound in the back of one of the men as he turned to run. Then Julien heard the rapid thunder of hoof beats as his comrades came riding in. He heard their shrill cries as they cut between the whites and the way station door.

He saw a man with a revolver in his hand come from the side of the way station, probably the one he had heard cursing out back in the corral. He raised his rifle and fired, and the man sat down, dropped the revolver, and put both hands to the hole in his chest.

Blue Stone was out of his saddle, running toward the way station door. The woman, trying desperately to close it, looked up and saw him. She screamed, a lost and awful sound.

But the sound did not stir pity in the heart of Julien Tremeau. He had heard it before, too many times, from the throats of the women slaughtered at Sand Creek.

Blue Stone's steel tomahawk buried itself in her skull. He yanked it back, red and dripping, and sprang through the door. Iron Horse followed him. The others pursued the whites into the darkness.

Temporarily alone, Julien ran around the way station to the corral at the rear in time to see a second hostler crossing the corral. The man ran in a shambling way, climbed the fence on the far side, and sprinted toward the trees that lined the riverbank.

There wasn't enough light to shoot, so Julien followed, running swiftly and tirelessly. He saw the white blur of the man's face as he turned to look behind. Then he was on the man and swinging his tomahawk with deadly skill, with murderous force.

The man went down, dead before he struck the ground. Julien stuck the dripping tomahawk into his belt, and drew his knife. It was the first scalp he had taken himself, although he had seen it done. A swift incision, a ruthless yank. He stuffed the scalp into his belt, picked up the man's revolver, and returned at a trot to the way station.

Bodies lay scattered like dolls before it. Julien knelt and quickly took the scalp of the first man he had killed. Then, stuffing it into his belt with the other one, he seized the fallen rifle and went inside, stepping over the bodies of the two women in the doorway.

His men were inside, ransacking the place. Blue Stone was sampling the food spread on the long table, making expressions of distaste each time he did. His hands were stained with blood that he had only partly wiped away.

Julien said: "We want guns and ammunition. Search the place and take every one you can find. Take powder and ball. Then when that is done, you can take trinkets for your squaws."

He watched them as they went from body to body, taking powder horns and bullet pouches, sometimes a belted revolver. He himself gathered up all the guns he could find and piled them on the table after sweeping it clean with his arm.

The braves brought the guns they had found and piled them on top of his. When they had finished, he carefully selected the best of the rifles and gave one to each of his men. He ignored the revolvers except to take one for himself. He yanked a blanket from a bed in one corner of the room and piled the powder and ball in the center. Then he tied the corners and handed it to Iron Horse. He got another blanket, dumped in the remaining guns, and gave it to Beaver. He headed toward the door.

He paused over the awkwardly sprawled body of one of the women. His eye caught by a small gold locket around her neck. On impulse, he stooped and yanked it loose.

He stood aside while his braves filed out. Then he crossed the room to the fireplace, reached in, and found a charred stick. On the table he scrawled his initials, *JT* and the number of killed, *11*. He went outside again.

His men had mounted and were waiting. They were jubilant and chattering like boys.

Julien stared with brooding eyes at the dimly lighted scene of death. He knew it wasn't pity that stirred his heart. Yet his feelings were not the same as the feelings of his men. He felt no

71

jubilation. He felt no joy. There was, instead, a kind of unpleasant sickness in him.

Impatiently he swung to the back of his horse, which Blue Stone brought to him. With his face set in hard and angry lines he led the way toward the southeast.

This had been different than killing Ludens, who he had hated fiercely for a personal wrong. It had been different than other battles he had been in with Pawnees and Utes. He had experienced no joy of battle tonight. It had been like killing chickens on his aunt's farm back East. Just a bloody, necessary job.

Necessary. In that word was the anger that smoldered so hotly in him. Why? Why was this slaughter necessary? Why had the slaughter at Sand Creek been necessary?

He shook his head with fierce self-disgust. He made his mind remember that morning at Sand Creek and the days that had followed it. He deliberately brought back the image of Bird Woman, and the faces of his children. He forced himself to remember that cage in the carnival tent, and imagined his children, dirty, terrified, imprisoned like wild animals while the people of Denver paraded past, staring into the cage with the impassive curiosity of people walking through a zoo.

Blue Stone shouted: "Black Dog, you are quiet! Are you not satisfied with the way we have fought tonight?"

"I am satisfied, Blue Stone. I was thinking of other raids. I was thinking of a band of warriors at my back ten times your numbers, a hundred times. I was thinking that we can drive these white vultures from our lands with their own guns that we shall take from them."

But he spoke the words by rote, and had to force conviction into his voice.

Their horses trotted through the night in single file, with Julien in the lead. There was no further talk. The moon came up, a yellow ball upon the eastern horizon. East of Denver, Julien halted briefly and stared at the clustered lights below where Cherry Creek joined the Platte.

Without speaking, he led away again at a slow and tireless trot. There would be dancing in the village tomorrow. There would be feasting and celebration. When he went out again, there would be more eager braves to follow him and less hesitation within the village.

Give him two more such victories as this, he thought, and he would have a band of fifty men. Then he could start riding to other villages and talking to other chiefs. His force would grow and grow, until even Chivington's army would flee from it. His name would become a curse that would strike terror in all.

The night was a soft, dark blanket over the land. The air was cold and the horses' breath blew out ahead of them in visible clouds. Sometimes they plowed through crusted snow lying in a ravine or in some place that was well sheltered from the sun.

Stars winked brightly overhead. The moon made a slow, majestic journey across the sky. The eight painted braves plodded along.

Dawn grayed the eastern sky. The sun painted the clouds pink and shining gold, and, as it rose above the plain, the victorious warriors rode into their home village.

Julien's face was fierce. He would not stop; he would go on. But the savage joy he had expected his vengeance to yield was missing. He was only tired and hungry and irritable. He only wanted to eat and sleep, and then go out again. He shook his head impatiently. It was only that his thirst for vengeance was too strong. Eleven deaths would not satisfy it, nor would ten times eleven. Only when he had driven the whites from the mountains and the plains could he feel satisfied.

Night Star greeted him at the edge of the village, running along with terror-stricken eyes until she saw his face. He had only a brief, cold nod for her. He rode to his teepee and swung down from his horse.

X

Night Star took his horse's reins from him and watched him stride through the teepee flap. Leading the horse and running, she went through the village and beyond to the edge of the horse herd. Here she turned the horse loose and watched while one of the boys, who was guarding the herd, drove it into the bunch. She returned, then, still running, carrying the bridle and Indian saddle the horse had worn.

She went into the teepee where a meal was cooking in anticipation of Julien's return.

He was squatting beside the fire, staring moodily into it. His face was angular and harsh. He did not look up.

Silently she ladled his food into a rawhide bowl and handed it to him. She moved away and stood behind him and a little to one side, silently watching him.

He showed the world only his harshness and his cruelty, but Night Star saw something else in him. She saw his continuing grief and his desperate loneliness. She saw his uncertainty.

She was his wife in fact now, even though he had not intended it to be that way. She would continue to be his wife, whenever he wanted her, even though she knew that, when he made love to her, in reality he was making love to Bird Woman, who was dead.

Bird Woman had been her sister and Julien's first wife. Night Star felt no jealousy because he still grieved for her. It was proper that he should. Night Star also grieved for her.

But she was his second wife, now privileged to do for him all the things that Bird Woman previously had done. Keep his teepee, make his moccasins and robes, cook his meals, bear his children. . . . She wondered if she was carrying his child now. It would be a time before she would know. But she hoped she was. If she could give him children to take the places of those he had lost, then his hunger for revenge might slacken. His hatred might cool. He might again be the Black Dog that Bird Woman had known, the laughing, lusting, happy man he had been before the Sand Creek attack.

Outside she could hear the celebration within the village—the shouting, the laughing, the triumphant, excited voices. But Julien just sat before the fire, staring into its graying coals.

After a time the entrance flap was flung aside and Julien's father entered. He glanced at Night Star, nodded briefly, then crossed the teepee to the fire, where he squatted, facing Julien. Night Star hurried to give him a bowl of food, which he accepted with a nod of thanks. He ate in silence until the food was gone. Then, speaking in Cheyenne as though he thought English might offend his son, he said: "I have just heard how you battled the whites at the stagecoach way station."

Julien didn't even glance at him.

Tremeau said: "Black Dog is your name among the Cheyennes. Treacherous Dog might be a better name for you."

Julien looked up, his eyes burning with anger. He said: "Did they fight with so damned much honor at Sand Creek? Do you give a rattlesnake a chance to strike before you step on it?" Julien had lapsed into English unexpectedly.

"Did I teach you that two wrongs make a right? Why do you think the soldiers at Sand Creek were so savage and cruel? Because every one of them knew of some butchery like that you committed last night. Every one of them was seeking revenge for it."

"And now I seek revenge."

"Are you blind? Where is the end to it? For last night's business the whites will also want revenge. And more Cheyennes will die."

Julien stared at him with smoldering eyes. "Water runs in your veins. What would you have me do? Sit like a squaw inside my lodge and wait while they cover the land like locusts and kill the game and murder Cheyennes until none is left?"

Tremeau didn't immediately answer, so Julien went on. "You did not see the cage in which they kept my children. You did not see their pale faces and dead eyes staring up from the grave. These are things that can be wiped from my memory only with blood."

Tremeau asked: "And what of you? You're an outlaw. You'll be hunted until you're caught. The people of this village . . . all Cheyennes . . . will suffer because you are one of them."

Julien said coldly: "Go away. I wish to sleep."

Tremeau stared at him for a long time. Then he got up and in silence left the lodge.

Julien also got up and went to his bed. He lay down and closed his eyes. Night Star asked softly: "Do you want me to come and lie with you?"

"No!" The answer was sharp and angry.

Silently she picked up a moccasin she was making and began to work at the intricate dyed-quill design she was putting on it.

Julien lay silently in his bed. After a while he began to snore softly.

Night Star got up and went to him. She gently pulled the covers up over his naked, painted chest. She stared at his face for a long, long time. It had softened in sleep and was now more like the face of the man she had known before the Sand Creek affair. But the ravages of the long months he had lain wounded were still visible in it. So was the weakness caused by the wounds, weakness intensified by lack of sleep and his exertions of the past night and day.

Would he ever love her as he had loved her sister? Would he, indeed, ever really want another woman? She felt a bleak hopelessness. Bird Woman had been very lucky to have the love of a man like this. But even if he never gave her what he had given her sister, she knew that she still wanted him. Even if he gave her nothing at all.

She went back to her moccasin but it held only part of her attention and thoughts. She glanced often at Julien's face as he slept. She started every time he stirred.

The day wore on. Occasionally a young warrior came to the teepee flap to see Black Dog. She turned them all away, telling them to return when he was awake.

They were recruits for his band, she knew. And he would welcome them. He would become a great war chief. He would go on from victory to victory until he was famous throughout the land.

Or he would die. A cold hand seemed to close around her heart. Silently she prayed in turn to Heammawihio and to Julien's harsh white God to watch over him and keep him safe.

In midafternoon she replenished the fire. She left the teepee and went to the stream for water. Returning, she put on some meat to cook.

He awoke at dusk and rose and went to the stream to bathe. He came back and dressed in the soft deerskins she had ready for him. He squatted before the fire and ate ravenously. Outside, the light faded until there was none at all except for that given off by the small fire inside.

When he had finished, he sent Night Star to bring Beaver to him, along with his other warriors and the loot they had captured the night before.

Night Star went out and ran with Julien's message to Beaver's lodge. Returning, she built a huge fire in front of the teepee so that Julien would have light. His warriors came, along with a dozen or so young men who hoped to join his band.

He dumped the captured guns upon the ground. There was

much excitement and much talk. Julien accepted most of the young men as recruits and distributed the guns among them according to age and eminence in the tribe.

From the edge of firelight the elders watched, and Julien's father, and the band's chief, Standing Moose. Disapproval was in their faces but they did not interfere.

Excited young braves did impromptu dances around the fire. Members of Julien's band who had participated in the way station attack stood in the fire's light and related, with gestures, all that had happened the night before. They praised Julien's cunning and courage, and they boasted of their own. They displayed the scalps they had taken and screamed defiance of the whites into the silent night.

A primitive, savage scene, but Night Star did not find it so. She watched from the teepee flap with quiet pride. This was her man. She would make him her man if it took her all her life.

The fire died and the warriors tired. One by one they disappeared into the darkness, after being told that tomorrow there would be another raid. And when they all had gone and the fire was but a bed of glowing coals, Julien came into the teepee himself.

He sat down beside the fire and for a long time stared at it. Then, as if just remembering, he found the locket he had yanked from the throat of the dead white woman and gave it to Night Star.

Pleased as a child, she held it up, allowing it to swing back and forth like a pendulum, catching and reflecting the fire's light. Her eyes shone.

Julien said almost unwillingly: "It is not as pretty as your eyes."

She glanced at him in surprise.

He said: "Come here."

Nervously she went to him and knelt before him. He took the

locket from her and examined the broken chain. He worked with it several moments and then unfastened the catch. He put it around her neck, leaning close to fasten it.

Night Star's heart beat faster. Glancing down, she could just see the locket lying against her brown skin close to the swell of her breasts. *Perhaps tonight,* she thought. She had detected shaking in his hands as he fastened the locket around her neck. *Perhaps tonight. . . .*

He got up abruptly and strode from the teepee without a word. She stared at the flap in dismay. Why had he gone so suddenly? Why, when for a moment he had seemed so close?

She sat down silently beside the dying fire. She stared at it. She knew why he had left her so abruptly. He distrusted the fulfillment and content that he was afraid he might find with her. It would dull the edge of his hatred for the whites. It would diminish his need for revenge. And if that were not reason enough, there was another, perhaps just as strong. He still loved Bird Woman and grieved for her. Taking her sister so soon seemed like a betrayal to him.

He did not return, so reluctantly she removed her clothing and lay down on her bed. In the faint light she stared at her strong, brown body.

It was a woman's body now, where a year ago it had been the body of a girl. It was a body that should please a man. Her breasts were full and firm, her thighs rounded and smooth and strong.

But he would not come back tonight. He would roam the chill plain and perhaps bathe in the icy stream to cool his need for her. She could feel tears of disappointment burning behind the lids of her eyes.

Somewhere in the nearly silent village she could hear the soft sound of a lute as some young brave courted his sweetheart from the shadows outside her father's lodge. She heard a dog bark. She heard the soft sigh of the wind at the peak of the teepee.

Smoke rose from the dying fire toward the smoke hole at the top. Cold, she burrowed into the soft buffalo robes and closed her eyes.

She slept. She dreamed that Black Dog came, naked and dripping and cold, to the lodge and stood by the fire to dry himself before coming to where she lay. She felt his hard, strong body against hers, his strong, hard arms around her, holding her so close she thought he would break her ribs.

She felt his mouth, and his warm breath, and she felt his hands running along her thighs and stomach and breasts.

She heard his breathing become short and fast and knew her own was equally so. And her arms went up around him and held him close to her.

In the dream she dreaded awakening for she knew she would find herself alone. But she did awaken and she was not alone. The dream was no dream but reality, and Black Dog lay close to her and her arms were around his neck.

His breath came fast and deep. This was not earth, she thought, but heaven, for nothing on earth could compare with this. Ecstasy mounted to an incredible pitch and minutes became seconds in her consciousness.

A star exploded in her body, and it was pain, and pleasure, and a gradual dying of the flames consuming her. She was hot, but it was pleasant heat and now soothing, and she felt closer to this man beside her than she had ever been before.

He knows that I am Night Star this time, she thought exultantly. *He is loving Night Star this time and knows that he is.*

But she did not speak, for to do so might destroy the spell. Soft and warm and quiescent, she lay in his arms while his breathing slowed and became regular again. At the last, just before he went to sleep, his hand came up and touched her face ever so gently and dropped away.

She lay awake for a long, long while, for to sleep would be to lose the joy she was experiencing. Tomorrow. . . .

But she would not think of tomorrow, or of the many tomorrows that would follow it. She would not think of him in battle, however glorious and prideful such thoughts might be. For when she thought of him fighting, she also thought of him dying, his life leaking out in a scarlet stream upon the ground.

Yet in spite of her determination not to think such thoughts, they came unbidden to her mind. She saw him lying on the icy ground, his face pale and bloodless as it had been that day at Sand Creek. She saw scores of white men, bearded and dirty, riding past him and firing their rifles into his body as they passed.

The warmth left her body and it suddenly felt very cold. She nestled closer to him, trying to recapture the warmth and peace she had known before.

It eluded her. Cold and awake, she lay all the rest of that night in the grip of growing terror. But when morning came, she greeted him with a smile. For she knew he must never guess her fear for him. She was the woman of a Cheyenne, of a Cheyenne war chief. His glory must be her glory, even if his death was also hers.

XI

Julien rode out at dawn, this time with twenty warriors at his back. And southeast, instead of north. There was another route the coaches took, called the Smoky Hill route. News of the previous attack probably would not have reached that far this soon.

Besides, it no longer mattered if it had. His force was strong enough and well enough armed to attack openly in daylight and still be victorious.

He maintained a steady pace throughout the day and through most of the night, arriving at the way station he had chosen in the early hours of the dawn.

This time he positioned his men around the place to wait for dawn. This time he was confident and sure.

Gray made a long, irregular line in the east before smoke began to issue from the tin chimney of the place. The door opened and a tousled-looking man wearing only pants and underwear came out to stand, yawning and stretching, before it.

No coach was in. The man got a bucket of water from the pump, took it back inside, then reappeared, wearing a shirt and carrying a gun.

He went to the corral behind the building and began to catch relief horses for the expected coach. He tied them in a line to the corral fence, which was made of poles.

Julien hoped his warriors would be able to contain themselves. This man could be killed and the way station looted or burned, but he wanted more than that. He wanted guns and he wanted gold. He wanted trinkets and bright cloth for the women of the village.

This time, when he returned, he knew opposition would have solidified. His father was already against him. By the time he returned the chiefs and elders would be, too. But gifts for them and for their squaws might lessen opposition to a point where it would be ineffective.

The sky grew light rapidly. Julien, from where he had positioned himself, could see the road in both directions. But the sun was a burning ball of gold, fully above the horizon, before he saw the dust of the approaching coach.

He waited tensely, prone behind a clump of brush. His hands gripped his rifle tightly. His face was a hard, cold mask.

The approaching dust resolved itself into a coach and fast-traveling teams. There were two men sitting up on the box, one the driver, the other a guard. A third lay on the coach top behind them and this one also had a rifle.

Armed they might be, thought Julien. And ready. But they had no chance. They were as vulnerable as the village at Sand Creek had been. They would die as quickly as the others had. The more guns they had the more loot Julien could capture for his men.

The coach came on and it was apparent to Julien even at this distance that the vigilance of the men relaxed when they brought the way station into sight.

The agent came out and stood before the door, watching the coach roll in. The distance narrowed from a quarter mile to a hundred yards, to fifty. Then the coach was pulling up in a billowing cloud of dust. The guard put his gun on the floorboard and started to get down.

Julien took a careful bead on the shoulder of one of the horses. He fired, levered, swung his point of aim to the guard. He fired a second time and the guard pitched off the coach to lie, unmoving, in the dust.

Julien's warriors were firing now, with less telling effect. The driver stood up and tried to whip his teams into motion, apparently only then realizing that one of the horses was down.

The man who had been prone on top of the coach flung himself off between the coach and the way station. One group of Julien's warriors leaped to their feet and ran screaming toward the coach. Another group, which Julien had instructed to conceal themselves in a dry wash with their horses, now came galloping from it, screeching like madmen. They cut, at a dead run, between the coach and the way station, swinging their tomahawks.

Immediately the outside door of the coach came open and terrified passengers began to pour from it. Julien stopped and fired carefully several times.

It was over, almost before it had begun. There was the mopping up, the killing of those who were only wounded, the taking of scalps, the counting of coups. There was the looting. There was no need, this time, for Julien to scrawl his initials upon the ground. His work would be recognizable from this day on. If he refrained from leaving his mark, he knew he would get credit for other killings he had not committed at all.

Surprise had served him well. He had only one wounded brave, and no dead. He had guns, more ammunition, trinkets and women's clothing in quantity for Night Star and for the other women of the village. He selected the best of the rifles, an almost new repeating Henry, and kept it as a gift for Standing Moose.

His men rummaged through the coach and baggage, looking for things they had missed. One by one and in small groups, they finally drifted into the way station to gorge themselves on the food that had been prepared for the coach passengers, the driver, and guards. Finished with this, they overturned the stove and left. Before riding away, they shot the coach horses and all the remaining horses in the corral that were too heavy for their liking. The others they loosed and drove ahead of them as they rode away.

Looking back, Julien saw flames and smoke leaping from the doors and windows of the place.

His men rode jubilantly, clowning like boys. But as the hours passed, they settled down to steady traveling. This way the day passed, and the night, and again, in early dawn, they arrived at the village.

Again there was celebration. Shouting squaws and children followed them as they rode through the village streets. Women squealed with pleasure at the clothing and trinkets. They dressed themselves in the white women's clothing and their antics drew the first smile in a long, long time to Julien Tremeau's harsh face. This time he did not immediately retire to his lodge, but watched, continuing to smile.

He went at last, in midmorning, to his own lodge to find Night Star waiting there for him. Gravely he gave her the presents he had brought her. As gravely she accepted them.

Her soberness puzzled him, but he did not speak of it. He squatted wearily before the fire and accepted the food she handed him.

She seemed to be waiting for something, and he understood what it had been when the teepee flap was flung aside to admit his father, Standing Moose, Apache Horse the medicine man, and several others, all elderly and of high standing in the village. Silently they grouped themselves around the fire. Silently they accepted food from Night Star.

He stared at his father, angered by the implied criticism contained in his presence here. He said, almost defensively, in English: "There was no treachery this time. We attacked openly and in daylight. But we defeated them."

"How many? Half your number? And how many of those were armed?"

Julien glared at him, disliking him with sudden intensity. He said harshly: "You speak of equality and fairness. Where is the fairness in war? Was there fairness and equality at Sand Creek?"

"It is time you forgot Sand Creek."

"I will never forget Sand Creek."

Charles Tremeau stared at his son. Julien met the stare defiantly. Tremeau said: "You are behaving like a fool. You went to school in Saint Louis. You have seen how numerous are the whites. You have seen their railroads and their armies. You have lived with them and know they do not lack courage in war. You have seen the way they can unite behind a cause and that is something Indians have never done. You know you cannot win. You are leading your followers to certain death."

"Perhaps Indians also can unite. Because something has not been done before doesn't prove it can't be done." Julien's temper was rising and his speech was clipped and sharp.

"You will not succeed. I will oppose you and so will Standing Moose and Apache Horse."

"You are my father. I had hoped you would be with me."

"I am also white. And I know there is only one hope for the Cheyennes or for any other tribe. They must learn to live with the whites in peace. They must learn to live as the white man lives. Then and only then will white men stop hunting them like animals."

"You would have them surrender? When did a surrendering army get more than the scraps from the tables of the victorious? I know as well as you do that the whites are coming and will own this land. But I can delay them for ten or fifteen years. I can force them to deal with the Cheyennes and the other plains tribes as equals and not as a defeated army."

"You do not operate as an army. You operate like wolves, attacking the helpless and the outnumbered. You will command no respect from anyone."

"I have just begun." Julien's eyes burned. "Soon they will send their railroads here. I will stop their railroads because I will make every mile cost them a thousand men. That will command their respect."

"Perhaps. But what of the villages, stripped of their fighting men? The whites will attack and burn them, one by one. And when that happens, how long do you think you can keep your warriors?"

Julien frowned. He knew this was the weak point in his plan. If he united the tribes, if he pulled warriors from the villages for his raids against the whites, he would leave the villages helpless and without defense. He knew the whites well enough to know that they would lose no time taking advantage of it.

He stared at Standing Moose. He picked up the Henry rifle and handed it silently to the chief. He said, watching the chief's expression carefully: "With guns like this the Cheyennes can drive the white men from the plains. I will get more of these guns until every Cheyenne possesses one. Are you for me or against me?"

Standing Moose worked the action of the gun. He raised it to his shoulder and sighted on the teepee flap. He took it down again. "I am neither for you nor against you. I will wait. I will see."

Julien stared triumphantly at his father.

Tremeau stared back, with neither anger nor defeat apparent in his face. He said, in English now: "Revenge is like acid, hoss. It'll eat you up until there's nothin' left. I'll stop you if I can."

"You can't stop me."

Tremeau shrugged. "I should have let you die." He glanced up at Night Star, standing behind Julien. He studied her for a long time and at last he said: "Damned if I know why, but she loves you as much as her sister did. What about her, hoss? What if the whites raid this village an' she gets killed?"

Julien didn't reply. He stared at the fire instead. He had thought himself beyond loving. He had thought himself invulnerable. But he knew, in this instant, that he was not. The thought of Night Star lying cold and dead was like a knife in his chest. Nor could he deny the probability that this village would be the first to be attacked. There were, among the whites, men who not only knew that he came from the village of Standing Moose, but knew also where the village could be found.

He stared at Standing Moose, switched his glance to Apache Horse. "The village must be moved. Not just once, but often. Look-outs must be placed upon the nearby hills and kept there day and night."

He saw a stiffening in the faces of both Standing Moose and

Apache Horse, and he knew he had not put the request diplomatically enough. Suddenly he glimpsed the difficulties he faced. In every chief, in every medicine man, he would meet with the same resistance he was meeting now. All were jealous of their authority. All would feel they knew best what was good for their people and all would resent suggestions from him. He said quickly: "I will attack the whites. I will bring loot to this village. Its safety is in your hands."

He saw that they were only partly mollified. He picked up his own repeating rifle and handed it to Apache Horse. "I will see to it that each one of the men who remains with the village gets a rifle like this. But this one is yours."

Apache Horse, who had been resentful over his gift to Standing Moose, now appeared satisfied.

Julien said: "You will support me, then?"

Neither man answered. In silence they got to their feet and filed from the lodge.

Charles Tremeau remained behind. He said: "Don't count on 'em, hoss. They're on the fence right now, but get whipped once and see where they stand."

Julien stared at his father with angry eyes. "And you will try to turn them against me while I am gone."

"I sure will. Call it off, boy. Take Night Star and find yourself some peace. You're goin' to be sorry if you don't." He watched Julien a moment, then turned and went outside.

Julien scowled. He had not expected defeat here in his own village, which had benefited most from his raids. Defeated here, how could he expect to gain support in other villages where he wasn't even known?

He didn't know. It would take time, he supposed, and victories. Not just small victories, either, but big, decisive ones.

Tomorrow he would go out again. He would stay out this time, raiding, looting, gathering new recruits. Only when his force was big could he achieve big victories.

XII

He was still angry when he rode out in the morning at the head of his band. He stayed angry throughout the day.

He had no definite objective in mind this time. He was simply hunting whites. He wanted scalps, and loot, but mostly he wanted to kill.

In spite of the apparent formlessness of his desires, there was a plan in the back of his mind. Raid he would, and kill he would, and loot when there was anything worth the taking. But he would also visit each Cheyenne village that lay anywhere near his course.

He left a swath of destruction westward to the mountains and along their foothills south toward the Arkansas. The first day he attacked and burned a settler's wagon, getting only an ancient rifle and two horses for his pains. That evening he attacked a stagecoach leaving Denver along the Smoky Hill trail.

Coaches, he thought, were the easiest of all. They were easily stopped and usually overturned by the simple means of shooting one of the horses. The passengers, driver, and guard were either badly injured in the crash and unable to fight, or else they were so shaken up that killing them was simple and quick and without much risk.

From the coach, he got a good rifle to replace the one he had given Apache Horse, a small chest filled with money, mostly gold, and several other guns.

They killed a deer before nightfall and built a large fire on which to cook it. They gorged themselves and danced themselves to exhaustion.

The next day yielded nothing, but the day following that Julien took them into a cañon leading up into the mountains where they attacked a small mining settlement and left it burning when they were through.

This attack yielded a dozen rifles, several revolvers, a quantity of ammunition, and a considerable amount of gold dust in leather pokes. It cost Julien two dead and one man badly wounded in the groin. He sent the dead and wounded back to the village, along with trinkets, guns, and ammunition, and went on south.

A Mexican family near Pueblo died at their hands and the smoke from their burning cabin caused an Indian alert in the settlement. Julien turned east along the Arkansas.

Cheyenne villages were clustered thickly here. Peaceful villages whose inhabitants had come to trade with the Bents. Into one such village he rode soon after the raid near Pueblo, to be greeted at the village edge by a mob of boys and more than a dozen barking dogs.

He led his men slowly through the village, while the following crowd grew larger. He rode directly to the teepee of the chief, and greeted him gravely. He dismounted and said: "I am Black Dog, of the village of Standing Moose. I have gifts of guns and ammunition for those of your young men who wish to join me."

The young men crowded forward eagerly until a sharp command from the chief made them move quickly back. Their faces showed resentment.

The chief said coldly: "I have heard of you. What do you want here?"

"I want your support. I want your young warriors who are not afraid to fight the whites. I want all Cheyennes to unite and make war upon the whites with the coming of spring. When I reach Bent's Fort, I will use the gold I have taken to buy more guns and ammunition. Guns that shoot many times. Those who join me now will get those guns. And knives. And steel tomahawks. We have counted many coups and have taken many scalps. We will take more. There is glory for all who join me now."

The chief said: "No. It is not good. It is true that our young men have also made some raids. But without my approval. And they will make no more."

Anger stirred in Julien. No longer addressing the chief, he turned and faced the crowd, directing his glance to the young men he hoped would ride away with him. He shouted: "I was at Sand Creek! The cannon sprayed the village with shot before The People were awake. I saw women and children fall to the ground while their blood gushed out and made puddles where they lay. I saw the white soldiers come screaming down the hill. They butchered my squaw. They stole my children and put them in cages for the whites to stare at as if they were animals. My children sickened and died, from cold and from lack of food. I hate the whites more than I hate anything else on earth. I will kill whites until I am killed myself. I want men to join me who also hate the whites, who also want to kill. There will be loot, guns and powder for yourselves, trinkets and cloth for your squaws. There will be scalps and coups to count. With me you will live as Cheyenne warriors were meant to live, not like squaws squatting before your teepees mouthing stupidities such as . . . 'the Cheyennes must learn to live with the whites.' "

He glanced at the chief to find him white-faced with rage. He yelled: "How many are with me?"

There was a chorus of shouts. The chief tried to make himself heard over the shouting and failed. Julien bawled: "I will wait at the edge of the village! I have guns and will get more! I want men with the hearts of men! All who are afraid stay behind!"

He swung to his horse without glancing again at the chief. He rode out at the head of his band, savage, proud, but hiding within himself a sense of failure in spite of the hubbub he left behind, in spite of his knowledge that he had probably doubled the size of his band.

Recruits he would get, and a certain success would be his. He would probably leave the Arkansas with more than a hundred well-armed men. But he wanted more. He wanted the chiefs supporting him. He wanted the bands to unite.

Unless they did, he could be no more than an irritating thorn to the whites. He could frighten and kill some of them, but he could not frighten or kill them all. He could slow the influx of whites to the plains but he could not bring it to a halt.

He waited at the edge of the village, and the young men who were joining him rode out, shouting and jubilant. He led them away and along the Arkansas and he visited, in the days that followed, the other villages that lay between the mountains and the fort.

On the third day he halted his men half a dozen miles from the fort. He washed the paint from his face and body in a stream nearby. He removed the scalps from his belt and laid them on the ground. Then, carrying only his rifle and the gold, he rode alone to the fort.

Already he had more than a hundred men. Already he had a formidable force. But he still had a feeling of failure, for in each village visited he had met with opposition from the chief.

Perhaps, he thought as he rode, he needed even more reputation than he had. There must be more attacks, more raids, more scalps and loot. There must be more evidence that it was possible, in spite of their numbers and strength, to drive the white men forever from the land. But it would take time.

He rode up to the gate at the fort and entered without being challenged. The stockade was crowded with both Indians and whites. There were Cheyennes and Arapahoes. There were Comanches and Apaches and even a few Kiowas. There were wagons and travoises and horses. There were piles of buffalo robes, and beaver pelts, and the skins of other animals. And a smell of whiskey and humanity, of hides and cooking meat, of tobacco smoke and leather, of horses and manure.

Unrecognized, Julien bought guns, and powder and lead. He bought tomahawks and knives and steel arrowheads. He spoke in the Cheyenne tongue and kept his eyes downcast so that the trader would not see their color.

But when he paid with gold he knew the man did not intend to let him leave with his purchases. Dropping pretense, he raised his head. He spoke in English now. "Don't call for help. Don't try to reach your gun. You know who I am, and you know I won't hesitate to slit your throat. We'll go out of here together and get a wagon. We'll load it up. Then you'll drive with me to where my men are waiting for me. If you do as you're told, you'll come back alive. If you don't. . . ."

The man said: "Tremeau. You're Julien Tremeau."

Julien didn't bother to reply.

The man said: "There's a thousand dollars reward for you, dead or alive."

"Want to try and earn it?"

The man shook his head violently.

"Then let's go get ourselves a wagon. You go ahead. I'll split your skull if you don't bring it off. I've got over a hundred Cheyennes outside. If anything happens to me, they'll burn this fort to the ground."

The man nodded. He walked to the door, with Julien following. Julien was careful not to give the appearance of threatening him. But he stayed behind.

The fort was a square. On all four sides there were buildings and storehouses and living quarters nestled close to the outside walls and in some cases two stories high. A wagon passed, empty, heading toward the gate. The man with Julien called: "Ramon!"

The driver halted the wagon.

Julien's companion said: "Let the wood go until later. I need the wagon."

"*Sí, señor.*" The driver turned the wagon and brought it back. He pulled up in front of the store.

Julien said: "He can help you load."

The man nodded. He beckoned Ramon and the two began to load the rifles, powder, tomahawks, and knives that Julien had bought. Ramon kept glancing at Julien uneasily.

When he had finished, Julien moved close to him. "Get up on the driver's seat. Drive out. If anyone stops us, you get a knife between your ribs."

The man stared at him with widened eyes. He licked his lips. "*Sí, señor.*" He climbed up and Julien tied his horse behind.

He beckoned the other man. "You get up behind. Keep your back to me and face the rear." The man got into the wagon and Julien mounted to the seat.

The thin winter sun beat warmly down upon his back. There was mud in some places inside the stockade and a drift of old snow against the walls of the buildings on the south side. The wagon threaded its slow and ponderous way through the motley crowd.

A bearded, buckskin-clad trapper stared hard at Julien, frowning. A trader in shirt sleeves and apron watched from the gallery of one of the stores, also frowning. Julien wished he had stationed his men closer to the fort. The wagon was slow and ponderous. If anything was suspected, even after they had cleared the gate, it could be overtaken easily.

They reached the gate and passed on through. Julien said: "Drive slowly until you get beyond that rise. Then whip 'em up."

"*Sí.*" Ramon's hands were clenched, holding the reins. A small muscle in his jaw kept tightening and relaxing.

Julien said: "You two had better hope nobody takes a notion

to follow us. If they do, you're dead."

"We're dead anyhow. What've we got to lose?"

"I have said you could go back alive."

The trader snorted. "If your pa was to say that, mebbe I'd believe it. But I don't believe it from a sneakin' murderer like you."

Julien's anger flared. "You sound like maybe you want to die."

The trader shrugged. "They's worse things, I reckon. One of 'em's bein' a turncoat renegade. Butcherin' women an' little kids like they was hawgs."

"I did not start that."

"No. Mebbe not. Your pa told me about your woman an' your two little kids. I kin halfway understand you turnin' mean over it. But it's got to stop some place. You're killin' people that had nothin' to do with Sand Creek. An' our side is goin' to be killin' Cheyennes that's got nothin' to do with you. Where the hell's it goin' to end?"

"With the white men moving out. Or with me dead."

"Then I hope they get you soon. That's all I got to say."

"If you don't shut up, you won't be around to see it."

The man was silent. The wagon rattled across the empty plain. It had gone nearly three miles before Julien saw the dust raising behind.

He didn't hesitate. He jumped to the ground and untied his horse. He cocked his rifle and shot the wagon horses with two rapid, successive shots. Then he vaulted to the back of his horse and thundered away. Ramon and the trader got down from the wagon and began to run in the direction of the dust.

Julien rode recklessly at top speed, until he saw his men coming over a rise in front of him. He pulled to a plunging halt, beckoning. They had been coming to investigate the shots, he supposed. The fact that they had might mean the difference between losing the load of rifles or keeping it. When they reached him, he whirled his horse and galloped away in the direction of the wagon.

He topped a rise and saw the wagon with its two dead horses sitting alone on the empty plain. He saw the trader and Ramon walking swiftly toward the galloping group of whites from the fort.

Julien's warriors were half a mile farther from the wagon than they were. But they outnumbered the group almost ten to one. Julien slowed and rode at an even trot toward the wagon. The other group reached the two walking and stopped. They appeared to be talking and arguing. They did not come on. Motionless, they watched while Julien and his men surrounded the wagon and unloaded it.

Julien watched, frowning. There was now no way for him to get arms other than stealing them. Bent's Fort would hereafter be closed to him.

But he had fifty brand-new repeating rifles. He had a hundred pounds of powder and two hundred pounds of lead. He had several dozen steel tomahawks and knives. He had more than a hundred well-armed men. Perhaps when he needed more arms he would attack Bent's Fort and burn it to the ground.

Riding away, he knew he should be satisfied, but he was not. He was an outlaw to the whites with a price on his head. He was, in a sense, an outcast to the Cheyennes. He had gained recruits, but he had not succeeded in gaining the support of a single chief. The war would go on, but he would need considerably more success, on a larger scale, before he could hope to unite the tribes.

XIII

The days grew warmer as Julien and his warriors ranged north and east across the plains. Streams ran bank-full and the snows in the lower mountains began to melt. As grass began to sprout, a light green sheen was visible on the slopes that faced the south. Time was growing short. An uprising, to be successful, should start in the spring. The Indians' horses were thin right now. But give them a few weeks on a lush new growth of grass. . . .

And the days were warmer, too. Occasionally it snowed, but after half a day under the warming rays of the sun the snow would disappear.

There was a supply problem incident to moving a hundred and fifty men rapidly across the plains from place to place. They consumed an enormous amount of meat. Julien had ten of his men out constantly, hunting for game.

They raided as far north as Julesburg, almost as far south as Santa Fe. They ranged from the mountains two hundred miles eastward on the plains. They acquired and kept a horse herd of almost two hundred head so that they could change when the horses they were riding grew tired.

In Denver, the price on Julien's head mounted as the days and weeks passed. It jumped from $1,000 to $2,000 and then to $3,000. By April, it stood at $4,000.

He and his band left ranches and stagecoach way stations a smoking rubble behind. His band continued to grow.

But his men grew weary of the pace he set for them. And so, one evening in early April, he led them to his home village, upon whose location Blue Stone and Beaver had kept him posted.

Only when he saw Night Star's shining eyes looking up at him from the crowd that came out to welcome him did he realize how tired he was. He had been pushing hard, perhaps too hard. It would be good to rest a while.

He had recovered completely from his wounds and the weakness they had caused in him. His body was strong and hard, but much too thin.

An expression in Night Star's face troubled him, but he did not speak of it. He gave his horse to one of the boys running beside him, and followed Night Star to his lodge. Reaching it, he said: "Something is wrong, Night Star. What is it?"

"Your mother, Black Dog. She is dead . . . since early this morning."

Shock touched him. And then shame. He had seen very little of her since the Sand Creek affair. He had known she was ill but had not realized. . . .

He strode hurriedly to the teepee of his father and pushed aside the flap. Charles Tremeau sat in the center of it, staring at the ashes of a dead fire. He looked up and made a thin smile. "Thought it might be you. I heard the commotion outside."

"Where is she?"

"I buried her."

It did not seem strange to Julien that his father had buried her. It was the white man's way and his father was white. In himself was a strange mixture of Indian and white, but he had buried his own children in the ground instead of in the crotch of a tree as a Cheyenne would.

He sat down across from his father. He was silent for a long time, remembering his happy childhood and the part his mother had played in it. He had learned many parts of the Cheyenne life from her. But when he began to grow up, his father had taken over. Returning from school in St. Louis, he had found the gap wider between his mother and himself. But she had been ill even then.

He raised his glance and stared at his father's face. It was drawn and gaunt and filled with pain. He realized suddenly that his father had loved his mother as deeply as he himself had loved Bird Woman.

Tremeau looked up and met his glance. "I haven't seen you

for a long time. How have you been?"

Julien shrugged. "All right. I have a band of nearly a hundred and fifty men. They are good fighters and are all well-armed. We have been successful, but I don't suppose you are glad to hear that."

Tremeau didn't answer him.

Julien said—"I need your help."—and surprised himself with the words. He had not thought he would ask help from his father. He had not intended to.

Tremeau's glance held surprise. "My help? For what?"

"I need the support of the chiefs and medicine men if I am to do more than I am doing now. I'm an upstart to them, with neither standing nor wisdom. That may change in time, but I don't have the time. The white men grow stronger every day in spite of the raids I make."

Tremeau shook his head. "I can't help you, hoss, because I think what you're doin' is wrong. I doubt if the chiefs would listen to me anyhow."

"They would listen to you."

Tremeau shook his head again. There was reluctant regret in his eyes.

Julien felt his anger rise. In his anger, he switched to the Cheyenne tongue. "Then I will accomplish it without your help, just as I have so far."

Charles shrugged. He seemed hesitant for a moment, but at last he said: "Mebbe it won't come to nothin', but there's some soreheads in the village here that're out to get you. Watch your step."

Julien glanced at him questioningly.

"Some of the older Dog Soldiers are jealous of your success. Apache Horse has been stirrin' 'em up. They just might try to get rid of you and take over your band."

Julien laughed scornfully. "Let them try."

99

Charles grunted: "I warned you. Maybe it'd been better all around if I hadn't said a word."

Julien said bitterly: "Thank you at least for that."

Charles didn't answer and at last Julien asked: "What will you do now? Will you stay here and take another wife?"

Charles shook his head regretfully. "Nope. I'm a white man and I reckon it's time I admitted it. I got me a ranch down on the Purgatoire. I guess I'll go down there and live in a house again."

Julien knew his father had been more white than he ever had, but he had not expected this. Charles said: "Give up your bitterness and come with me. There's enough land for both of us and someday it will all be yours. Maybe I can square you with the government. I can try at least. With enough gold you can do damn' near anything. Bring Night Star with you. Raise some more kids and you'll eventually forget the way the others died."

A certain regret touched Julien and his expression was more human than it had been in a long while. But he shook his head. "I have made my choice. I will not change my mind now."

Charles watched him steadily for several moments. He shrugged. "Guess you won't at that. How long you stayin' here?"

"Two or three days."

"I'm leavin' tonight." He put his hand across the dead fire and Julien took it. Charles said: "Good luck, hoss."

Julien nodded. He got up and left the teepee, depressed by the realization that the old ways, the old days were gone. The free, happy life he had known so briefly had passed. The future could bring only conflict and hunger and pain. No matter how confidently he asserted that the whites could be driven out, he knew it wasn't true. Not unless the tribes united, and he knew that was virtually impossible. So it could be no more than it had been so far. Raids and killings and the burning of buildings. Eventually he would be hunted down and killed.

It was dark when he went outside. In the center of the village there was a huge fire around which many of his men were dancing and shouting. He supposed he should join them but he didn't feel like it. Nor did he feel, just now, like going to Night Star.

His thoughts were depressed and bleak. He walked out into the darkness away from the village. There had to be some way of achieving what he really wanted—a united uprising of all the tribes. If he could just do something big, something that would shock the whole country, something that would make his name known and respected at all the council fires. . . .

The village sat on the bank of a small stream. Behind it there was a bluff, thickly covered with cedars and brush. He climbed the slope leading to the bluff, and halfway up stopped and sat down to stare broodingly at the fires in the village below. Night Star would be waiting for him and would be hurt when he didn't appear. But he didn't move.

Somewhere near him a mouse scurried through the dry grass, making a rustling sound. On top of the bluff a coyote howled, to be answered by barking from the village dogs.

He got up and strode restlessly down the slope, scowling to himself. He reached the bottom. . . .

A sudden coldness touched his spine. There was a rustling sound on his right, another on his left. He snatched his tomahawk from his belt.

His father's words were suddenly repeated by his thoughts. There was jealousy among some of the older Dog Soldiers. Apache Horse had been arousing them.

A form came rushing at him from the darkness and a tomahawk whistled past his head only inches away. He leaped back like a cat, then sprang forward swinging his own tomahawk with deadly precision as he did.

He recognized the man even as he closed with him, even as

he felt his steel tomahawk bite through scalp and bone. It was Running Antelope, whose brother had been killed in Julien's raid on the mining camp.

A body struck him from behind and the sharp edge of a knife pierced the skin above his ribs. But he pivoted as it did and the knife glanced off, penetrated between skin and ribs for a couple of inches, then was withdrawn for a second strike.

He seized the knife wrist with both hands and yanked. He brought the man toward him, off balance, then swiftly shifted the hold of his right hand to the elbow. Driving the captive arm down, he raised a knee beneath it as he did.

The arm struck his knee violently and he heard the bone snap. He flung the man away and leaped back.

A rifle roared, no more than half a dozen feet away. The bullet tore through the surface muscles of his thigh, dumping him neatly to the ground. The rifle roared again, but this time the bullet whistled past several feet above where he lay.

He doubled convulsively and rolled to his hands and knees. The one with the rifle was silhouetted for him in the light from the village fires. He came on up to a crouch, drew back his arm, and threw the tomahawk, recognizing his target as he did. It was Apache Horse.

Blade forward, the tomahawk struck him squarely in the face, drove him back and down. Drawing his knife, Julien whirled to face two others now coming at him from behind.

At the sounds of Apache Horse's rifle, the revelry had come to an abrupt halt and now the village was as silent as the night surrounding it. Then Julien heard the sounds of swiftly running feet.

The two facing him hesitated. One raised a rifle to his shoulder. Julien pivoted and flung himself to one side. He pivoted again and drove forward. His body struck the thighs of the man with the rifle just as it discharged. Then he was down and Julien was wrenching the gun from his hands and driving his knife in deep.

The other one disappeared into the darkness, unrecognized. The running feet came closer and an instant later Julien was surrounded by his men. He heard a swift scuffle, a yell of pain from the man with the broken arm. After that there was only silence.

He got to his feet. Some of the men carried torches, pieces of wood snatched from the fire and burning only at one end. In this flickering light he saw Apache Horse and Running Antelope, and Three-Legged-Badger lying dead on the ground. The fourth, who he had just killed, was Broken Bow.

Blood ran from the gash along his ribs and from the bullet wound in his thigh. He stood, head down, breathing harshly and rapidly.

He felt no pleasure at seeing his assassins dead at his feet. He felt no pride. He felt weak and weary, and sick.

His men chattered and shouted and praised him for his feat. But all Julien could think was that five men of his own village had hated him enough to want him dead. All he could think was that his own people, who he had thought to help, agreed with him so little that they would try to kill him.

In this moment, failure was a sharp, bitter taste in his mouth. He pushed his way through his men and headed for his teepee.

Night Star found him at the edge of the crowd and ran a little ahead of him all the way to the lodge. Arriving, she quickly built up the fire, then came to him and helped remove his blood-soaked clothes.

She dusted powdered mescal buttons on the wounds to kill the pain. She gave him others to chew. He lay back and let her work on him, feeling weakness come and go in waves.

His physical wounds were hurts only of the flesh. They would not incapacitate him and they would heal. But there was a wound in his soul that would not heal. It would fester and swell and grow putrid with decay. His own people had betrayed him. The men of his own village had tried to murder him. Many months would pass before he would be able to forget that perfidy.

Blue Stone brought the weapons taken from the dead men to the teepee and carried them inside. Without much interest, Julien looked at them.

All were weapons he had given them. The rifle with which Apache Horse had wounded him was his own rifle, presented to Apache Horse as a gift.

He closed his eyes and held them tightly closed. He tried to quiet the turmoil in his mind and failed. One terrible question kept repeating itself in his mind. *Were the gods, Heammawihio of the Cheyennes and the God of the white men—were they against him?*

Until now he had thought what he was doing was right. But now he wasn't sure.

XIV

It was not altogether the pain of his wounds that kept him awake all through the night, but it was partly that. He lay, unmoving, on his back, staring at the patch of night sky visible through the smoke vent at the top.

Beside him, Night Star breathed softly, asleep. Outside, the noise quieted and finally died.

His father had come, earlier, to see if he was all right and to tell him good bye. Then he had gone, leaving forever the village where he had lived so many years, where his son had been born, where his wife had died.

Julien had seen the pain of that farewell in his father's eyes, perhaps because he was uncertain and in pain himself. For a moment, while Charles stood there looking down at him, he had wanted desperately to ask counsel from his father, and almost had. But he had kept his lips locked, mostly he supposed because he had known what his father's counsel would be.

There must be someone, some place, to whom he could go. He knew that among the Cheyennes it was a custom that when a man was troubled he went alone to a high mountain top and there went without water or food until he had talked with the gods.

His white education told him it was primitive superstition, that hunger and thirst eventually brought on a kind of delirium in which the man saw visions conjured up by his confused and troubled mind. Yet his white training also told him that it was prayer of the most sincere kind. Perhaps the visions were not caused by hunger, thirst, or delirium at all. Perhaps they were God's way of answering the prayers.

He got up quietly, wincing with the pain of his wounds. He dressed in clean deerskins and moccasins and, with no weapon other than a knife, he stepped out into the clear, chill night. The teepee flap moved behind him. Looking back, he saw that Night Star had followed him out. He said softly: "Go back to sleep. I will return in five days. Tell my warriors I have gone to seek the counsel of Heammawihio and that they are to wait for me here."

"I will tell them."

He tipped up her face and stared into it. Then he turned and strode away toward the place where the horse herd was.

He called out to the young men with the horses as he drew near so that they would not mistake him for an enemy. He took the horse they caught for him and slipped his bridle on. He swung to the animal's bare back.

He rode westward without haste, ignoring the sharp pains that the horse's movement caused in his side and leg. When dawn came, he was close enough to the mountains to see them clearly, their dark shadows of pine, their brown, bare slopes, their snowfields higher up. He continued to ride all through the day, slowly and without haste, but he was careful to ride in low places so that he would not be outlined against the sky.

That evening he stopped and gave his horse an hour to graze. Afterward he went on.

Again he spent the night riding, and, when dawn came the next day, he was climbing through the scrub pine that covered the foothills crowding against the plain.

So far he had taken neither food nor drink. Late that morning he climbed his horse to a rock-strewn mountain top that looked eastward for a hundred miles and westward to the high, icy peaks of the divide. And now, at last, he tied his horse and slept.

It was a troubled sleep, in spite of his weariness. A sleep filled with troubled dreams in which he was an outcast both to whites and to Cheyennes. All were against him; all were trying to kill him. He fought, but he went down in defeat before their superior numbers. Each time he would wake just before he was killed and would find his body bathed with sweat.

He awoke at dawn. He got up and wandered aimlessly about on his mountain top. Not yet would he pray to the gods for help. Not yet.

He cared for his horse, leading the animal down to water at the stream in the valley below. Returning, he tied the horse to a low clump of brush so that he could graze.

He was both hungry and thirsty when he returned to the rocks at the mountain top. The air began to warm and the sun beat steadily against him. This was Ute country, he knew, and Utes were mortal enemies to Cheyennes. So he kept close watch upon all the surrounding hillsides.

The day wore slowly on. Time after time he relived the years he had spent in the East while he was going to school. He remembered in detail his long trip West, ending when he found his father and his father's village.

The sweetest memory of all was that of his courtship of Bird Woman and the early years of their marriage. Those had been the good times, he thought, the times that now could not again return.

However he tried to reject the belief, he knew the Plains Indians and their way of life were doomed. It was only a matter of time. The history of the whites was one of inexorable movement West. That of the Indians was one of inexorable retreat before the oncoming tide. Other tribes had attempted to slow the advance, but all had failed. He also would fail. However he fought against the admission, he could never really avoid it.

His mouth dried up and his lips cracked. His tongue began to swell. He looked at the tumbling, clear stream in the valley. He imagined what it would be like to bury his face in it and drink.

He looked away and out across the plain again. On the nearest hillside a small bunch of deer came into sight through the pines and underbrush.

The deer would disappear and so would the buffalo. That, he supposed, was the thing that would finally and completely defeat the Indian tribes. Take away their food and you destroyed their ability to fight. It had happened in the East and it would happen here.

The day wore on. The sun dipped in the western sky and began its long trek down. It blazed briefly, lighting the clouds with orange and gold, then slipped behind the mountains in the west. The dusk came, as gray and gloomy as Julien's brooding thoughts.

He shivered with the cold. He lay down on the cold ground and stared up at the stars. He felt light-headed and weak.

To which god should he pray first, he wondered. Or did it matter? Perhaps there were not two gods, one for Indians and one for whites. Perhaps there was only one, his image simply different to the different peoples. No one had ever seen him and so no one could know what he was like.

He would pray, then, assuming Heammawihio was the same god as the one worshiped by the whites.

He closed his eyes. Confusion reined in his thoughts and he prayed that the confusion be dissolved, that he learn, one way or the other, what he should do.

No answer came to him nor had he expected one. Not yet.

He continued to pray. The cold sharpened. His body stiffened with it, and the cold spread through him until there seemed to be no warmth in him at all. He lay as though he were dead, his eyes open and staring at the stars.

A pattern began to emerge from them. He saw first an enormous man, his face stern and harsh, and this one seemed to be white for he had a bushy beard like a patriarch. This one scowled down at Julien, his eyes filled with disapproval and dislike.

Julien thought: *I am only half white, but tell me what the white half of me must do.*

The stern eyes of the star image said to him: "Stop. Stop the slaughter of innocent people."

Julien's voice was weak and cracked but he spoke aloud. "No. I will not stop."

The face was terrible in its wrath. Julien began to shiver violently with an eerie kind of fear. He felt as though he had invaded a realm in which he had no right. He half expected lightning to slash down out of the clear sky and pin him to the ground.

But nothing happened. He closed his eyes, and, when he opened them again, the image was beginning to fade. Or change. The face seemed to be softening. The beard seemed to dissolve and disappear.

The nose was larger now and was the strong, hooked nose of a Plains Indian. The face was smooth, but just as strong as the other one had been. Braids seemed to appear on either side of the enormous head. Julien knew this was Heammawihio, god of the Cheyennes.

Again he asked his tortured question. But this time the great eyes looked at him with understanding and with sympathy. They seemed to say: *The Indian has been wronged and you must fight to right the wrong.*

Julien could not have said whether he replied aloud or whether his reply was in his thoughts. *I will fight. I will go on fighting. But how am I to earn the support of the people for whom I fight?*

The great eyes seemed to be weighing him, weighing his sincerity and his strength. *That will come to you. But you must do a thing that will be known from one end of the white man's land to the other. Then and only then have you a chance to do what you want to do. Then and only then will the tribes unite.*

What thing? What great thing must I do?

The face began to fade. Julien tried desperately to hold it in his thoughts, but failed. Little by little the image disappeared and again became the separate stars winking coldly in the velvet sky.

Julien got stiffly to his feet. He paced back and forth to warm himself. He thought of the water in the valley, then forced his thoughts away from it.

He paced restlessly for more than an hour until his body began to feel warm again. *That will come to you,* Heammawihio had said.

Or had the god said anything? There had been no sound that his mind remembered. There had only been the restless, cold sighing of the wind in the pines. There had been only the roar of the tumbling stream lifting from the valley below. There had been only the lonely wail of a coyote on a distant peak.

The words he had heard had been in his mind but that did not mean they were imagined words. God did not necessarily speak to men as they spoke to each other.

A great thing. He must do a great thing that would be known from one end of the white man's land to the other. But what great thing? What thing could he do that would be so widely heard and known?

Sporadic attacks on ranches and stagecoaches and way stations would attract little notice in themselves. But if he attacked and burned a town—a large town—even Denver perhaps. . . .

That was it. Elation touched him and excitement stirred his blood. He must attack Denver and burn it to the ground. He must stop slaughtering whites by tens. He must slaughter them by hundreds all at once.

Destruction of Denver would be reported in newspapers all the way across the land. It would be talked about. It would make others among the whites who were planning to come here afraid. It would make the hearts of all white men turn cold with fear. For if a large settlement like Denver could be destroyed, it would mean that no settlement was safe.

Even more important than the reaction such a feat would cause among the whites was the reaction it would have among the tribes. They would take heart; they would believe that anything was now possible for them. They would greet Julien when he rode into their villages as they greeted a great chief. They would listen to his words. The chiefs and medicine men who now held back because they did not believe resistance was practical would change their views. The tribes would unite. A horde of warriors would roam the land, plundering, destroying, killing. The land would be bathed in blood but it would be white blood.

How long he paced back and forth upon his mountain top,

he didn't know. Dawn came unnoticed to the sky. The sun poked above the horizon.

He hurried to his horse. He rode down into the valley and dismounted at the stream. He drank and bathed, and scraped the whiskers from his chin with the razor-sharp edge of his knife.

Mounting, he rode swiftly eastward, down out of the mountains and across the plain. He rode as swiftly as his horse would go and paid little attention to concealing himself.

He had a plan at last, a plan that would work. If he succeeded, and he promised himself grimly that he would succeed, he could avenge Sand Creek in a single night. The whites would learn what it was like to awake from a sound sleep to find murder stalking them. They would see their own women and children slaughtered and bleeding in the streets. They would learn what it was like to be caught unarmed and pursued to extinction by men who were as merciless as Julien's men could be. They would learn what it was like to be hurt and cold and to lie dying while they prayed for help that never came.

Julien shouted with jubilation at the sun climbing up the flawless sky. Then he sobered as he realized how much planning such an attack would take.

It could result in destruction for the Indians as easily as it could result in the destruction of the settlement. It could mean final and ignominious defeat for him and his band of men.

Yet even here the advantage was with him. He looked as much white as he did Cheyenne. His eyes were gray, as no Indian's ever were. He could dress himself as a white man, cut his hair, shave, and go to Denver to scout out their defense. He could find their weaknesses and their strength. And then, when all these things were known, he could attack.

He hurried. The hopelessness and despair he had known before were gone. The attack on Denver was going to be the beginning of the end for white settlement on the plains. With Denver a smoking rubble, the tide of whites could do nothing but recede.

XV

He arrived at his home village in the middle of the following night, a different man than he had been when he left. He was ravenous and weak with hunger. He did not wait for Night Star to serve him the food that was slowly simmering over a nearly dead fire in the center of the lodge. He seized the pot and began to eat from it with a bone spoon.

Night Star came and freshened the fire. She brought him water, which he gulped greedily. She sat down across from him and watched, her eyes pleased at the change in him.

She said: "You have talked with the gods."

He nodded. After so long a fast, the sudden gorging made him a little sick. He stopped eating and took a short drink of water.

Night Star did not press him further, but he had to tell someone and so he said: "I talked with both the God of the whites and with Heammawihio. The God of the whites did not like what I was doing. But the Cheyenne god told me that I must do something that would be noticed from one end of the white man's land to the other. I will attack Denver and burn it to the ground."

Her eyes widened with fear. "Is that not too dangerous?"

He laughed. "Perhaps. But I have a hundred and fifty men. When the Cheyennes learn what I intend to do, that number will double. If the city is attacked suddenly and without warning, as they attacked us at Sand Creek, three hundred men will be enough. Besides, I intend to go to Denver alone, dressed as a white man. I will count their numbers and plan an attack so that it will be possible."

"When will you go?"

"As soon as it is light. Find me the white man's clothes I wore last time I went there."

She got up silently and went to look for them. Julien picked up the pot of meat and began to eat again, more slowly now.

During his long fast his wounds had scabbed and begun to heal. They still bothered him, but not as much as they had before. His mind raced excitedly. He envisioned Denver, the proud city of the plains, lying a smoking rubble with its people dead. He saw himself riding at the head of his victorious band of warriors, attacking one settlement after another until none was left. He imagined all the Cheyenne, Arapaho, and Sioux villages joined and knew that they could, between them all, put ten thousand warriors into battle. No white man would dare set foot upon the plains. Not for another fifteen or twenty years.

When he had eaten his fill, he lay down and tried to sleep, but excitement was too strong in him. At last the daylight came, showing itself first as an oval of gray at the teepee peak.

He got up and went outside. One of his warriors saw him and shouted for the others. The shouts echoed from one end of the village to the other, and, before the sun had begun to rise, all his warriors were grouped around him, waiting to see what he would say.

He stood before them and shouted: "I have a plan that will drive the whites forever from the plains! This morning I will dress myself in white man's clothes and go to Denver to scout their defenses and their numbers. Each of you must go to his own home village and there recruit one man. Come back immediately when you have done so. I will return as soon as I can . . . in four days at most. There must be three hundred warriors waiting for me when I do return."

They shouted approval in excited voices. Julien waited until the shouting had died down and then yelled: "I have the ap-

113

proval of Heammawihio for what I plan to do! We cannot fail!"

Again shouting swept the village. Julien turned and reëntered his teepee. He stripped off his deerskins and dressed himself in white men's clothes. Before a small mirror he cut his hair as best he could, knowing most trappers did the same. He picked up a white man's saddle taken in a raid, carried it out, and put it on his horse. He swung to the animal's back.

His warriors shouted at him as he rode out through the village. Night Star ran along beside him, looking up at his face. At the village edge, he leaned down and touched her smooth hair briefly with his hand. "Do not worry about me now, Night Star. Nothing can touch me. When this is over, we will have a time of peace and then we will raise those strong sons we want."

There were tears in her eyes as he rode away. In spite of his reassurances, her expression was strained with fear for his safety.

He rode steadily and without haste, again toward the mountains but bearing north this time. And he rode with care, for he now must watch out for his Indian brothers instead of for the whites.

He stopped at nightfall and allowed his horse to graze for an hour. He ate of the dried meat Night Star had given him and drank water to wash it down.

Weakness had fled from him. Purpose and hope had strengthened him. His wounds scarcely bothered him. He felt strong and alive again.

When the hour was up, he mounted and rode all through the night. In early morning he stared at the growing city nestling on the plains.

The land rose eastward from the town, climbing in a gentle grade. He could see the ribbon of silver that was the Platte and the other, narrower one that was Cherry Creek.

It was a big town, but it had no stockade, no defenses of any kind. It should be easy for them to ride through it, killing and burning as they went. There was only one real danger—that the city might be warned.

Alerted, they could station men with rifles in the upper windows of the buildings. They could barricade the streets. They could slaughter the Cheyennes as they piled up at the barricades.

He sat his horse on the hill east of town for more than an hour, staring down and studying it. The main streets seemed to run roughly parallel to the Platte and perhaps half a mile away from it. The river bottom was filled with cottonwoods and brush, with little gulches and sloughs. The attack must come from that direction, Julien thought to himself, instead of from this, where his warriors could be seen long before they reached the town. And in early dawn, in the first gray light of day. White men did not rise as early as Indians did. Early dawn would catch most of them in their beds. A night attack would not be practicable where there were so many buildings. His men would not be able to see their sights.

Slowly he rode down the slope and into the town. The sun had been up for more than an hour and the place was busy now. Heavy freight wagons rumbled through the streets behind their heavy teams. There were all kinds of smaller rigs, and men on horseback and men on foot.

Julien circled the town and rode toward the riverbed. The trees were beginning to put out leaves and the ground was green with grass. He rode south along the Platte, carefully planning the route by which he and his men would enter town.

There were several small cabins in the river bottom. In front of one a woman was washing clothes while two small children played nearby. Julien avoided going very close.

He rode south past the ferry, then turned and retraced his steps, consciously marking the best route in his mind. At the edge of town he stopped again. People flowed past him, scarcely noticing him.

He would have to split his band, he decided, and send about fifty up each street. The first shots would bring the whites out into the streets. By the time they understood what was going on and began to set up some defense, half of them would be dead.

Fire must become the Cheyennes' weapon when the white men holed up in their buildings. He thought: *The fires must begin at twenty or thirty different places on the outside edges of town at the same time the attack begins. Burning toward the center, the fires will drive the whites in that direction and trap them there. Flames and smoke will finish the job the Cheyennes had started. Those who escape and run to the edges of town will be finished off with ease.*

To Julien, it was a tactical problem that involved no pity for the people who would be slaughtered. There had been no pity at Sand Creek. Why should there be pity here?

He rode up and down the streets, counting the people he saw. There were many times three hundred, he realized. But not all of them were men and not all the men were fit to fight. Some were too old; many were too soft; probably a third of them had never even held a gun in their hands.

Suddenly he stopped his horse. The animal fidgeted, made nervous by all the unfamiliar noise. Julien stared.

Half a block away he saw a man—there could be no mistaking him. But what was he doing here? He had told Julien several days before that he was going to his ranch on the Purgatoire.

Perhaps he had come here for supplies before going south. At any rate, Julien could not afford to let his father see him. Not here. Not now. His father would certainly guess from his presence what was in his mind.

He tried to edge to the side of the street but a freight wagon was in the way. He saw his father's head turn toward him.

He swung his horse so violently that the animal reared. A

buggy, pulling past the freight wagon, veered sharply to miss him and the driver cursed. Julien scowled at him. The man looked away. Julien moved behind the freight wagon and stayed there, keeping it between him and his father.

He had better get out of here. His father's presence reminded him that, although there were not many who could recognize him, there were a few. The trader and the Mexican who had been at Bent's Fort. A few trappers who had known him well. The newspaper editor—the doctor who had cared for his children—the old man who had buried them. A few only, but if one of them recognized him. . . .

The wagon rumbled up the street. Julien's horse pranced nervously beside it, trying to bolt but held by Julien's iron grasp on the reins.

Julien eased ahead a little in anticipation of drawing abreast of the spot where he had seen his father. And then, so suddenly that he had nothing to say, he was face to face with his father, who had started to cross the street immediately in front of the wagon.

Tremeau's eyes widened with surprise. His lips formed his son's name. Julien met his gaze harshly, steadily, as though daring his father to give the alarm and thus betray his own son to those who hated him.

He reined his horse around his father's frozen form, never letting his glance waver. Then he was past, and waiting with held breath for his father's shout.

Where did his father's greatest loyalty lie? With the whites who were his friends and of whom he was one? Or with his son, turned renegade and murderer, who could be riding the Denver streets for only one reason—that of scouting its defenses preliminary to making an attack on it?

Half a block fell behind, a block. No shout of alarm rose. Julien's breath sighed out with deep relief. He continued on to the edge of town and beyond, onto the open plain. Only then did he feel safe. Only then did he look around.

The town lay behind him, its nearest streets empty of galloping horsemen. His father had not betrayed him though he must have known why he was there.

He wished he had not seen his father at all. He'd had no desire to put Tremeau into such a position—that of being forced to choose between two loyalties. Nor could he be sure that his father's first choice, made so hastily, would be final. Tremeau might, on sober thought, decide he owed it to the people of Denver to warn them.

He halted his horse. He knew what he ought to do. Return to Denver now, before it was too late. Eliminate the chance that Denver might be warned. He had a little time. His father had not given the alarm when he rode past him on the street. It would probably take several hours for him to make up his mind. But if he were dead . . . ?

Julien's belly turned cold at the thought of murdering his own father. Such an act was contrary both to his white and Indian upbringing. And yet. . . .

He scowled fiercely to himself. He stared angrily at the town. Why had he had to see his father at all? In a town that size, why?

He started back, then halted his horse again before he had gone a hundred yards. He hesitated, angry at himself because hesitation was unlike him. He had chosen a course for himself. He would follow it until he died, doing all the things that must be done.

Except this one thing. He could not do this. Not cold-bloodedly and without feeling. His father had given him life. He had saved his life after the Sand Creek attack, when Julien would have died.

It was Julien who now was torn between two loyalties—to his

men, who he would be leading into a trap if his father betrayed him to the whites—to his father, who had done so much for him.

An impossible choice, but one he had to make. He sat motionlessly on his horse for a long, long time, scowling bitterly at the town he had sworn he would destroy. Twice he started back toward it and twice he stopped.

Suddenly he whirled his horse and galloped away toward the southeast. He did not look back.

XVI

It was a shock to Charles Tremeau, seeing Julien, dressed as a white man, riding brazenly through town. He stared at first in disbelief.

Julien's return stare was hard and uncompromising, challenging and cold. Charles had the feeling that if he cried out, Julien would unhesitatingly put a bullet through his chest.

Why was he here? Had he come for further personal vengeance against someone else he thought had been connected with his children's deaths?

He doubted it. But if it was not that, it could be only one other thing. Julien was planning an attack on Denver and had come to scout it out.

In that moment, Tremeau found himself imagining Julien's bloodthirsty warriors riding through the Denver streets, killing, mutilating, burning.

A teamster yelled at him and he hurried out of the way and across to the far side of the street. From the walk, he stared after Julien. Wrong, his son might be. But that would not help the hundreds he would kill if he ever attacked Denver in force. Nor would the destruction of Denver be the worst consequence. If Julien had such a victory to boast about, he might well realize his dream of uniting all the tribes.

119

Julien passed from his sight and his chance to give the alarm was gone. Slowly, thoughtfully he walked to the Elephant Corral. He had a choice. He could take his teams and wagons loaded with the supplies he had come here to buy and leave. He could drive southward to the Purgatoire. He could forget that he had seen Julien and guessed what Julien intended to do. Or he could go to the authorities in Denver and alert them to the peril they were in.

Either course was a betrayal—the first of his own people, the second of his only son. Either course was intolerable.

There was only one thing to do. Alert the Denver authorities. Then go to the village of Standing Moose and tell Julien what he had done and try to persuade him to abandon his ambitious plan.

He frowned bitterly. Why did there have to be such continuous and unremitting warfare between Indians and whites? There was room enough in this vast country for both of them. But they were too different, he supposed. They had no understanding of each other and wanted none.

He paused at the gate leading in to the Elephant Corral, hesitated, then decisively turned and headed toward City Hall.

It stood near the bank of Cherry Creek. He went inside and along the hall until he reached the mayor's office. Again he hesitated, his hand on the doorknob. Then, resolutely, he went inside.

The mayor was a bearded man, dressed in a business suit. Tremeau took his hand. "I'm Charles Tremeau."

"The father of . . . ?"

Tremeau nodded. "The father of Julien Tremeau."

The mayor's expression was harsh. "What do you want from me? An amnesty. Pardon for that renegade? I can tell you right now that the answer is no."

Tremeau shook his head. "I came to warn you. I saw him

here in Denver not fifteen minutes ago."

"And you didn't . . . ?" The man stared at him unbelievingly.

Tremeau said: "No. He's my son. He saw his wife murdered at Sand Creek. His children were caged in that carnival tent until they sickened and died."

"You're not justifying the things he's done?"

"I'm neither justifying the things he's done nor the things that were done to him. I'm simply warning you. I think he came here to scout the town's defenses preliminary to attacking it."

The mayor's face lost color. "Good God!" He stood frozen for several moments, then hurried toward the door. "Maybe we can still catch him."

Tremeau said: "I doubt that."

The mayor whirled. "You let him get away. You know what he's done and what he is. I ought to throw you in jail and charge you with being an accessory to his crimes. For all I know you are."

Tremeau's voice was softly dangerous. "I wouldn't try it, Mister Mayor."

For several moments the two stood glaring at each other. The mayor's eyes lowered first. He grumbled: "All right. I guess, if you were in it with him, you wouldn't have come here at all." He looked up. There was reluctant respect in his glance. "It must have been a very hard thing for you to do, Mister Tremeau. How much time do you think we have?"

Tremeau shrugged. "I wouldn't plan on any more than three days."

"Will you stay until I can get the commandant here from Camp Weld?"

Tremeau shrugged. "Don't know why not."

"Thank you." The mayor hurried from the office. After a few moments Tremeau heard a horse gallop away. The mayor returned. "I've sent for him." His face was shocked. "Good

God, Mister Tremeau, when I think of what that bloodthirsty renegade could do. . . ."

"Maybe he won't try."

"What kind of defense do you think we could set up?"

Charles said dryly: "Something better than Black Kettle had at Sand Creek."

The mayor flushed. "I guess we deserve that, Mister Tremeau. For whatever it's worth, though, there were a good many people in this territory who deplored what Chivington did. It was inexcusable."

Charles shrugged.

"Now that you've warned us against him, what do you plan to do? Surely you don't intend . . . ?"

"To let him ride into a trap? No. I'll go out to his village and see him. I'll talk him out of it if I can."

"What if . . . ? I mean a white man isn't exactly safe out there on the plains right now. Suppose you don't reach him?"

"I'll reach him."

"And afterward? Do you think for a minute he'll let you leave, after what you've done?"

Charles shrugged fatalistically.

"Where will you go if he does?"

"I've got a ranch down on the Purgatoire."

"And what about him? We'll get him eventually, you know."

Charles grinned wryly. "Don't count on that."

The mayor frowned. "I was thinking. . . . Mind you, I don't know if everyone would agree to this, but if he could be persuaded to leave the territory, perhaps an amnesty could be arranged. Not, of course, if he goes through with this Denver attack."

Tremeau stared hard at him. "Do you mean that?"

"I'd be willing to work on it, Mister Tremeau. You understand, though, that I'm only Denver's mayor. Governor Evans would have to approve. So would the Territorial Legislature. It might never go through."

Tremeau heard a rattle of horse's hoofs outside the City Hall. He heard the pound of boots in the hall. The door flung open. A uniformed man with captain's bars on his shoulder came in, followed by several others of lesser rank.

The mayor said: "Captain, this is Mister Tremeau, father of Julien Tremeau."

The captain swung his head and stared sharply at Tremeau.

The mayor said: "He tells me he has seen his son in Denver. He believes his son means to attack us."

"He wouldn't dare."

The mayor smiled. "Think, Captain. Just because Denver is big doesn't mean it is invulnerable. We have no defense, no stockade of any kind except the little one at the Elephant Corral. He not only would dare, but, without being warned beforehand, he might very well succeed in destroying us."

The captain nodded grudgingly. "Give me twenty-four hours. After that he won't have a Chinaman's chance."

The mayor nodded. "Very good, Captain. I'll leave it in your hands."

The captain nodded again. He stared at Tremeau. "Want me to throw this one in the guard house? Or are you going to keep him here in jail?"

"Neither, Captain. Mister Tremeau has done nothing wrong."

"He sired that god-damned renegade. Ain't that enough?"

Tremeau got up. His thumb was hooked in his belt, close to the butt of his gun. He said: "Captain, I don't like you. Open that big mouth of yours once more and I'm going to shut it for good."

"You bastard. . . ."

The mayor jumped between them. "Gentlemen, for God's sake! Aren't we in enough trouble without making more?

123

Captain, Mister Tremeau is to be allowed to leave Denver when he wishes. Is that understood? He intends to go out to his son's village and try to talk him out of the attack."

"If the son-of-a-bitch will betray his own son, do you think he won't betray us?"

"Captain!" The mayor's voice was a roar. "Get out of here and do what you're supposed to do!"

The captain glared at him for several moments, tall, lean, with harsh blue eyes and a thin-lipped mouth showing through his clipped brown beard and mustache. At last he said: "Yes, sir."

He went out of the office, followed by his men. The mayor said: "I'm sorry, Mister Tremeau. Perhaps you'd better leave now before the captain gets things organized."

"All right." Tremeau shook his hand briefly and went out. He walked along the hall and out into the spring sunshine. He stood for several moments, motionless, staring down the street.

He had the terrible feeling of having done something irrevocable. He had a depressed feeling of guilt. He had betrayed his own son.

Why couldn't he have just ignored Julien's presence here? Why couldn't he have ridden out in silence?

He shook his head. That would have been a worse betrayal than this. He would have felt personally responsible for every death Julien caused when he did attack—the women, the children, the helpless. He had done the only thing he could, but it was bitter all the same.

He walked slowly to the Elephant Corral. His wagons were ready, except that the teams had not yet been hitched to them. His two men, Manuel Vigil and Joe Smith, were sitting comfortably against one wheel. Tremeau said: "I'm not going back with you. Get yourselves a couple of men that can scrap if they have to and get started. I'll see you on the Purgatoire."

"*Si, señor,*" Vigil said. Joe simply nodded in his wordless way.

Tremeau crossed the corral and got his saddle horse. He swung to the animal's back and rode out through the stockade at a walk. He scowled thoughtfully and worriedly as he rode eastward through the town.

Julien's reaction to the news of what he had done would be violent. He expected that. Julien would probably attack him. He expected that, too. What he couldn't predict was what he would do himself when it happened. Would he defend himself, killing his own son if necessary to keep from being killed himself? Or would he stand passively and permit Julien to kill him unopposed?

He could find an answer to neither question. Instinct might force him to defend himself. But to kill his own son. . . . His face twisted, as though from pain.

He left the town and started out across the plains. He knew every inch of them, every landmark, every drainage, every river and creek. He stopped at a high point of land a mile from the town and stared behind.

Bells were ringing. People were scurrying through the streets like busy ants. Already preparations for the city's defense had begun. When Julien arrived, if he did, he would find that he had been cheated of his greatest advantage—surprise. He would find a system of alarms, probably the same bells that were ringing now, ready to warn the town of his approach. He would find barricades set up across the streets to stop his galloping warriors and force them either to retreat or fight on foot. He would find, instead of decisive victory, overwhelming defeat.

His plan, if Charles was guessing right, to unite the tribes by giving them such a major victory, would be defeated once and for all. He would be finished as a war chief, and could henceforth be no more than a raider with a small band of diehard followers. He would eventually be hunted down and killed.

But there was another choice for Julien and perhaps, when this was over, he would take it at last. He could give up his fanatical thirsting for revenge. He could ride south with his father to the ranch on the Purgatoire. Even if an amnesty could not be arranged, he could live in relative safety there, surrounded by loyal *vaqueros*. He could bring Night Star with him and raise another family to take the place of the one he had lost. He could find peace and satisfaction.

Charles spurred his horse. Everything depended, now, on how Julien took the news that Denver had been warned. Everything depended on how persuasive he could be when he told his son.

How much, he wondered, did Julien really want to unite the tribes and drive all the whites from the territory? How much did he want peace, and Night Star, and a chance to raise more children? Charles realized with mild bitterness that he didn't really know. Since the Sand Creek affair, he had never gotten very close to Julien. But he hoped that there was, in Julien, a growing kind of disgust for his own corrosive bitterness. He hoped that the heady excitement of warfare had not yet taken too firm a hold on him.

He would know soon, he thought. He should reach the village of Standing Moose by tomorrow morning if he traveled steadily all through the night. He should reach it only a few hours behind Julien.

He tried to feel hopeful, but he failed miserably. An overwhelming feeling of hopelessness and despair began to grow in him for he knew how great were the odds against success in what he hoped to do.

XVII

Julien reached the village in early dawn but The People were already up and waiting for him. Besides the main horse herd belonging to the village itself, there was a second horse herd, the mounts of Julien's old band and of the new recruits.

Forty or fifty of them rode out to meet him, racing their mounts, whooping excitedly. Their faces and chests bore bizarre streaks of red, yellow, and blue paint. In their hair they wore eagle feathers, one for each coup they had counted. Shouting, yipping, they galloped in a circle around him as he rode into the village, only stopping when the teepees and The People got in their way.

Julien could see that nearly all his men had done as he had instructed—each had brought another man. His band had grown and now numbered almost three hundred.

He rode directly to his lodge and found Night Star waiting before it, watching him as he approached with shining eyes and a welcoming smile. He dismounted, and, because he felt exuberant, he snatched her from the ground and swung her around. She laughed delightedly.

He went into the lodge and stripped the white man's clothing from his body. Night Star brought him deerskins and he put them on. He had no braids, so he did not bother with feathers. Nor did he take time to smear his face and chest with paint.

Excitement filled him as he thought of the impending attack. He hugged Night Star briefly and almost absently, then went outside to be surrounded immediately by his men.

He said: "Come. We will plan the attack."

They followed him out beyond the edge of the village, talking excitedly among themselves.

Julien stopped and shouted at them: "Form a circle around me so that all can see!"

The circle formed. Julien drew his knife. Bending, he drew an irregular line on the ground from north to south. He said loudly: "This is the Platte." He drew another line, this one joining the first one from the east. "Cherry Creek." He began to draw regularly spaced lines at the confluence of the first two, and, when he had finished that, drew others at right angles. "The streets."

He stepped back from his work and took a lance from a nearby brave. Using it as a pointer, he drew a lighter line along that representing the Platte and approaching from the south. "We will approach this way, just before the dawn. There is brush and trees, and many small sloughs between the river and the town. We will be well concealed. When we reach the town itself, parties of fifty men each will go up each street. Others, in groups of two and carrying live coals with them, will set fires in the wooden buildings along the edges of the town. The whole town will catch fire, but it will burn from the outside in, driving the whites not already killed toward the center of it. We will kill them as they run through the streets trying to escape from the fire."

He glanced around at his men. An involuntary cheer went up, a cheer that lasted several minutes. Two or three braves on the inside of the circle did a sudden, exuberant dance.

Julien stared at Iron Horse, then switched his glance to Blue Stone. "What do you think, my brothers? Is my plan a good plan? Will Denver be destroyed?"

Both men nodded solemnly. Iron Horse said: "We cannot lose. But we must travel toward Denver with care so that no news of our coming goes before us."

Julien said: "This we will do. And we will travel swiftly, so that, even if we should be seen, those seeing us cannot reach it before we do."

Dead Buffalo asked: "When do we go, Black Dog? Today?"

"When the sun is high. We will go when the sun is as its highest point in the sky."

Julien looked at Comanche, the young medicine man who had been with him from the start. "Go out on a hill and make good medicine for us. Speak to the sun and the sky and the earth."

Comanche nodded and pushed his way through the group. Julien raised both hands for silence. He roared: "Attire yourselves in your best! Paint yourselves for battle! Care for your weapons and catch the best horses that you own! Go now, and do well all the things I have told you!"

Shouting, running, talking excitedly the men dispersed. Julien watched them go. There was a strong feeling of elation in him as there was in each of his eager men. He had planned well. He had a strong force of men not afraid to die. They were well mounted and well armed. Their fanaticism was exceeded only by his own.

They would not lose. They would leave Denver a smoking rubble, stinking of the dead. Thinking of it, his heart thumped rapidly in his chest.

Something made him look around and he saw a horseman approaching from the west and north, and even at this great distance there could be no mistaking him. It was Charles Tremeau.

Motionless, Julien watched while the figure approached. Some of his men might have gone out to intercept, but when they saw Julien watching the figure, they held back.

Tremeau rode directly to Julien. He halted. Without speaking, he let his glance roam and take in the feverish preparations that were under way. He said regretfully: "Then I guessed right. You are going to attack Denver."

"I will not only attack it. I will destroy it." Julien's voice was strong and sure.

Tremeau's face was haggard and gray with fatigue. He dismounted stiffly and spoke in English. "Guess I ain't as young as I used to be. I'm plumb played out. Reckon that nice little woman of yours could give an old man something to eat while he catches his wind?"

"You are welcome in my lodge."

"Let's go, then. After I've eaten, we can talk."

"There's nothing to talk about."

Tremeau shrugged. Leading his horse, he walked stiffly toward the village. Julien paced beside him.

A strange uneasiness began to grow in Julien, driving away the elation he had previously felt. He scoffed at it and attributed it to weariness. After all, it had been two full days since he had slept more than an hour or two. But it persisted in spite of his scoffing.

He knew his father was going to try to talk him out of the attack. He also knew he would not listen.

Reaching the lodge, he held aside the flap while Charles entered. He followed his father in.

Night Star greeted Charles with shyness and respect, and obviously with great liking. Tremeau sat down exhaustedly, cross-legged, beside the fire. Julien sat down across from him. He stared at his father broodingly. Tremeau seemed to be having trouble keeping his eyes open.

Charles asked, while Night Star prepared a plate of meat for him: "How've you been, hoss? Them wounds all right?"

"They are healing."

"Good." Charles began to eat ravenously. He did not speak again until he had finished and had swallowed some of the water Night Star handed him. He stared at her thoughtfully until her face turned pink, then glanced at Julien. "Think again, hoss, about my place on the Purgatoire. It'd make a real fine home for you an' her. You could raise a dozen kids if you wanted that many. It wouldn't be too bad a life for you, either. You'd be out in the open all the time, ridin', workin' the cattle. But if you go through with this attack on Denver, you'll be finished as far as ever livin' in Colorado is concerned. They'll hunt you down no matter where you go."

"When the attack on Denver is finished, they will not be hunting anybody down. They will be running for their lives."

"Don't be too sure of that. I know you think you've got a sure thing, but nothin's sure, believe me. There's a lot of people in Denver. There's a fair-size bunch of soldiers at Camp Weld. They just might cut your bunch to pieces."

Julien shrugged. "That is a chance a man takes when he chooses to fight."

Charles's eyes sparkled suddenly with anger. "Damn it, don't be so bull-headed! You're throwin' yourself away, that's what you're doing! The mayor of Denver. . . ." He stopped suddenly.

Julien stared at him. "What about the mayor of Denver?"

"Nothin'! I was just going to say that the mayor of Denver and a lot of other folks just might agree to an amnesty for you if you'd give up this crazy scheme."

"That is not what you meant to say."

"The hell it ain't."

"You have been talking to the Denver mayor?"

Charles said angrily: "What if I have? Right now the mayor and the governor and everybody else would agree to an amnesty if you'd just get off their backs. They've tried catchin' you, and that hasn't worked. Now I figure they'd be willin' to buy you off with just about anything if you'd give the whole thing up. But raid and burn Denver and you're through. They'll hunt you down and they won't give up."

"I could not change my mind now even if I wished. My warriors would say my heart was that of a squaw."

Charles eyes drooped, but he forced them open determinedly. "The hell they would. Nobody doubts your courage. All you got to tell 'em is that your medicine ain't good. Go out on the prairie a couple of hours an' try to make medicine. Come back and say you've failed, that you saw a crow die in mid-flight, that you saw a black dog lying dead, that a strangely shaped cloud obscured the sun. They won't doubt you and you know damned well they won't. Tell 'em that and then we can load your stuff on a travois an' be on our way."

Julien wavered for a moment, but only for a moment. When he looked back at his father, his eyes were blazing. "You would make an old woman of me! You would have me betray those who trust in me. You would have me lie to save my own skin. These things I will not do!"

He got up angrily and, before Charles could speak again, strode through the teepee flap and out of the lodge. He heard his father call his name, but did not stop. Furiously he strode through the village and out onto the prairie. He saw Comanche on a rise not far away, and walked toward him.

His father's words had been true, he knew. He could still call off the Denver raid. All he needed to do was to say his medicine was bad. It happened frequently. He himself had once gone on a horse-stealing raid against a Pawnee village. That raid had been called off within sight of the village horse herd simply because a hawk had dived and caught a mouse between the raiders and the horses they meant to steal. Nor had there been any dissension among the braves. They had all returned to their home village, convinced that the raid would have been disastrous if they had gone through with it.

Yes, he could call off the raid. He could go with Charles to the ranch on the Purgatoire.

He kicked a rock savagely. He stopped, turned, and stared at the village, now humming with activity. Out near the horse herd a dozen braves were galloping, wheeling, making imaginary passes at an imaginary enemy.

He smiled faintly and his eyes glowed. It was a barbaric and colorful scene that he would not be likely to see too many more times. His face clouded at the thought and his eyes lost their glow, becoming troubled. Why had he thought just now that he would not be likely to see such a scene too often again? If they were victorious in Denver, he would see it many times. Only if they were defeated overwhelmingly. . . .

He whirled angrily. His medicine was bad, all right. His confidence and assurance were gone. But he wouldn't stop. There was no reason why he should, no reason a white man's logic could understand.

He climbed the knoll and joined Comanche at its top. The medicine man wore a headdress made from buffalo horns. His face was painted garishly. Julien asked: "How is your medicine?"

"It is good, Black Dog. We will win. We will take many scalps and capture much loot and many guns. We will return to the village in triumph and every band on the plains will join together to drive the whites from our land."

Julien nodded and turned away. He smiled ruefully to himself. Comanche had told him what he knew Julien wanted to hear. He no doubt believed it himself. But the core of uneasiness still hung in the back of Julien's thoughts.

He sat down on the ground and stared broodingly at the village below. He tried to rationalize his own uneasiness. It was caused . . . it must be caused by the enormity of the task he had set himself. Denver was a giant compared to his small force.

But it was a weak giant, he told himself forcefully. A weak giant that could be killed.

The sun climbed up the nearly flawless sky. The warm spring sun beat against his back and the smell of awakening earth and growing things filled his nostrils.

Slowly his confidence began to return. He stared up at the sun and sky and prayed to Heammawihio for its full return. He got up, then, and trotted toward the horse herd half a mile from the village edge. He took a horse from one of the young men who guarded the herd and swung to its bare back. Then he thundered toward the village, joined by a score of shouting, galloping braves. He wheeled, and galloped with them on an imaginary foray, shouting as excitedly as they.

His eyes shone as he broke away and went toward the village again. His confidence had returned. He was ready to go and he would not fail.

The sun was almost to its zenith now. His men were beginning to gather. He galloped through the village to his lodge for his weapons and saddle.

His father had fallen asleep where he sat, obviously the deep sleep of complete exhaustion. He got his things quietly and went outside again. He told Night Star good bye and mounted his horse. Then he went to where his men waited for him and led them, shouting, toward their planned objective.

He had been gone nearly an hour before Charles awoke. He did not know that Charles immediately caught the best horse left in the village and pounded after him. He and his men were traveling too fast for Charles ever to eliminate that hour's lead, particularly with the horse he had.

XVIII

They rode steadily throughout the rest of the day. Gradually their exuberant spirits calmed, but their confidence did not wane. And as they progressed steadily toward their objective, Julien's own doubts began to fade. He had planned the attack carefully. The advantage of surprise would be with him. He could not fail.

Darkness fell across the land, and, when it did, they halted for a brief rest, no longer than twenty minutes. Afterward they went on again, loping the horses for about half an hour, then walking them half that length of time.

They traveled in utter silence. There was only the soft thunder of their horses' hoofs, the metallic ring of weapons and ac-couterments, the heavy breathing sounds of their hard-pushed mounts.

Familiar landmarks passed. It was still completely dark when Julien passed a bluff that told him they were now less than a mile from the city's edge.

He moved into the lead, cautioning his men as he passed among them to complete silence. Magically the sounds of hoofs seemed to soften. The metallic clang of weapon against weapon ceased. Even the breathing of both men and horses seemed to grow still.

Along through the cottonwoods and brush lining the Platte he led them, taking advantage of every wash and slough, of each bit of cover he could find. The distance separating them from the edges of the town dwindled to less than three hundred yards.

Now he moved among the men, separating them into groups of about fifty each. The two-man teams who carried live coals in mud-lined containers broke away from the main band, to right and left, and began to surround the town. Julien tried to relax, but his nerves and muscles were too tight for relaxation. He waited, measuring the time it would take the fire teams to reach their appointed places.

He did not dare move until they had. But he must move before any of them were discovered and the town alerted.

The minutes seemed to drag. The sky was still completely dark, though there seemed to be a lighter streak lying along the horizon to the east. The horses fidgeted, their riders' tension seeming to communicate itself to them.

The streak in the east became more pronounced. In another ten minutes, Julien thought eagerly. . . .

A burst of rifle fire in the distance broke the silence shock-ingly. Undismayed by it, Julien raised an arm and screeched: "Go, my brothers! Attack now!"

Again there was the thunder of hoofs, but this time it was not soft. It rolled toward the silent town in a rising crescendo, accompanied now by the shrill, sharp cries of the eager Cheyennes.

They swept upon the city like a wave, guided now by several flickering fires growing along the farthest edges of the town, by the sounds of volleying rifle fire, by the sharp, distant cries of some of the fire teams that had been caught and forced to fight.

More light, Julien thought desperately. They needed a little more light. Had he miscalculated by sending the fire teams in too soon? Would he be defeated because his men could not yet see to fight?

A fire in a nearby frame shed licked up its walls and crowned the roof, lighting everything for three hundred yards around. Leading his own group of fifty men, Julien thundered into a hard-packed street.

He did not see a single white. There was not a glimpse of movement along the street.

More light! his thoughts cried. *More light!* And even as they did, he realized that the grayness in the east had spread across the sky. He could see the silhouettes of the buildings against it. He could see well enough to shoot, but there was nothing at which to shoot.

He cursed savagely in English under his breath. What had gone wrong? There was enough noise now to wake the whole damned town. . . .

As though in answer to his desperation, bells suddenly began to peal. And, staring ahead, he saw something vague and indistinct stretched across the street.

He did not slow his pace. As he thundered along, the barricade became increasingly plain to him and he could make out empty wagons placed end to end so that they reached across the entire street from building wall to building wall.

At almost the same instant he realized what constituted the

barricade, a withering volley of rifle fire poured from beneath it, from between the wagons, from over the tops of them.

Horses reared beside him and behind him, and fell to the hard-packed street in a flying tangle of hoofs and bodies. Warriors were thrown, and spilled, but the wave of attack neither slowed nor stopped. Others surged from behind to take the places of those who had gone down.

The bells pealed almost frantically now. The few fires that had caught blazed brightly in the growing light of dawn. Julien could see the faces of the men behind the barricade. Their numbers were unbelievable. There must have been a hundred and fifty behind the barricade in this street alone.

Again that ragged, deadly volley rattled out. Julien's horse went to his knees, throwing Julien over his head. He rolled in the street, stunned.

The whole street was now filled with grayish light. Enough to see each plank, each window and door in the buildings on each side. Enough to see that the barricade had been placed far enough inside the town to insure complete annihilation of the attacking Cheyennes. For there was no way they could escape. There were no openings between the buildings here. There was no cover of any kind. The only route of retreat was back down the street the way they had come in, exposed to that murderous, withering fire from behind.

He had been betrayed, he thought. Somehow, some way the city had been warned. They had not prepared this kind of defense in a matter of minutes or hours. This had taken days.

Who had betrayed them? Julien knew the answer to that immediately. His father had. His own father had warned the town and caused this bloody massacre.

Of his fifty men less than a dozen now remained. Prone behind dead horses in the street they were returning the fire coming from behind the barricade with courage and determination but without very much success. Julien himself lay behind the twitching body of his own horse, trying with frantic desperation to think of some way in which he could yet snatch victory from defeat. Unwounded horses were bolting away down the street toward the river bottom.

Several, though, confused by the fire and guns, milled back and forth up and down the street. As one of these passed close to him, Julien leaped to his feet, threw an arm around the horse's neck, and swung astride.

Immediately he swung himself to the side of the horse that was away from the barricade as the horse thundered diagonally away. The firing increased in intensity, but miraculously the horse escaped being hit.

Others who were still alive followed Julien's example. A block from the barricade he hauled the horse to a halt and stared behind.

Five men rode out. Five out of the fifty that had ridden in. It was butchery. White men carrying guns streamed out from behind their barricade. They moved among the wounded Cheyennes lying in the street, callously finishing them off.

The bells continued to peal. The fires mounted and spread. Julien heard the crackling of the flames, and smelled the acrid smoke that lay like a pall across the town.

Defeat. Its taste was bitter, sour in his mouth. In less than ten minutes the glorious force he had been so sure would win had been virtually annihilated. If he rode away from Denver with fifty men, it would be a lot. He would leave more than two hundred and fifty dead behind.

For several long moments he considered leading his men in a suicidal attack upon that barricade. If some of them could get through. . . .

But he shook his head reluctantly. Even if half a dozen Indians did get through, they could accomplish nothing by doing so.

They would be cut to pieces before they had gone a hundred yards. The buildings immediately behind the barricades were filled with sharpshooters in case any Cheyennes did get through.

Down the street he could see another tiny group of stunned survivors, and farther still another group. He swung his head and looked the other way. He saw half a dozen others riding toward him, slowly, dazedly, as though unaware of the bullets still being fired at them.

Julien raised a hand. He gestured toward the Platte. He waited until they all had turned, then rode slowly that way himself. He looked with unbelief at the sky. There were a few high, pink clouds floating in its gray expanse, but the sun was not yet up.

How many minutes, he wondered, between the first gray light of dawn and sunrise? Fifteen at the most. In fifteen minutes his band had been wiped out. The glorious victory that was to have been his was gone. Gone, too, was his dream of uniting the prairie tribes.

He was finished. He would henceforth be known as bad medicine among the Cheyennes. It was doubtful if he could recruit another brave, or even keep the few he had.

In this instant, shock was uppermost. He swung his head and stared dazedly back toward the burning town. He could see the men who had been behind the barricades running around with buckets and axes trying to extinguish the flames. A long line—a bucket line—had already been formed between one fire and the creek.

He halted his five beneath a cottonwood half a mile from the edges of town. They were as stunned as he and had nothing to say. They just stared apathetically at the town and at the stragglers riding toward them from it.

Julien counted. Five were with him. He could count another fourteen. They reached him, but he waited still for any others who might ride clear.

Four men, probably survivors from the fire teams, approached him from the left. Another seven came in from the right. And that was all. He waited until the sun had been up almost thirty minutes before he reluctantly turned away.

Thirty men. Thirty-one, counting himself. And an hour ago there had been three hundred, armed and eager, sure they were going to win.

Except for one, he had lost all of his original tiny band. Blue Stone was gone, and Rain Cloud, and One-Eye. Dead Buffalo and the young medicine man, Comanche, were also gone. Only Iron Horse lived, and, unless he had aid soon, even he would not live. His right arm was a shattered mass of blood and torn flesh. Blood ran along it and dripped steadily to the ground. His face was gray, his eyes filled with pain, his expression one of stoic endurance.

Julien led them swiftly away to the south, staying in the river bottom where there was cover in case they had to fight again. Half a dozen miles from town he halted, and moved among his men, giving them all the aid he could. He tied Iron Horse's arm up with deerskin bandages to stanch the flow of blood. He did the best he could with the wounds of half a dozen others.

And then he led them on, not leaving the river bottom until he could travel through a narrow strip of rough country leading east.

For a while, he could see the pillar of smoke rising from the town of Denver far to the left. But eventually that dwindled and died away as the residents brought the flames under control. Julien's mouth twisted bitterly. He had failed even in this. He had not even succeeded in burning the town.

He had hated before. He had thought his hate stronger than that ever felt by another man. He had hated all white men for the thing they had done to the Cheyennes at Sand Creek.

But he found that now his hate was even stronger than it had been before, perhaps because it no longer encompassed all white men but had centered itself upon only one. The one whose treachery had caused this awful disaster. The one he called Father. The one he now must kill if he ever expected to erase the taint of shame from his name.

It was torture to travel for those who were wounded. Julien was forced to halt often throughout the day so that they could rest. If he had not, they would have been unable to go on.

He kept watching behind for pursuit, but none materialized. The fires, he knew, had kept them from pursuing him. Though they were under control, the residents did not dare leave. Embers undoubtedly still glowed, embers that a wind might fan into another conflagration larger than before.

No. There would be no pursuit. He would reach the village of Standing Moose with his men. He would rest and eat and sleep. Then he would take up his father's trail. He did not for a moment believe he would find his father still in the village of Standing Moose.

And he would stay on that trail, no matter how long it was, even if he was forced to stay on it for weeks, for months, for years.

His father would die for his treachery. He promised himself that. What happened afterward no longer mattered to him. Killing his father had become the only goal he had.

XIX

It was a pitiful remainder of the once splendid force that straggled back into the village of Standing Moose. And it was a subdued, shocked group of villagers that watched as they slipped from their horses and stumbled into their teepees.

Two of those from other villages came with Julien to his lodge and collapsed to the floor, overcome with weariness and with the pain and weakness of their wounds.

Outside, there was a great wailing from the women who had lost their men. Julien said: "I am not hurt, Night Star. Take care of these two who are."

He closed his eyes and tried to keep them closed long enough to sleep, but there was to be no sleep for him. Not yet. Not until he stopped seeing the awful butchery on that Denver street. Not until he stopped hearing the cries of the wounded and dying, the savage, unending volleying of the white men's guns.

With his stare steadily upon the smoke hole at the teepee top he asked: "Where has my father gone?"

Night Star's voice was scarcely audible. "He followed you on the fastest horse in the village as soon as he awoke and found that you had gone. He was very excited and said something about having to reach you before it was too late. But you must have been traveling too fast for him to overtake you. He came back late last night, got his own horse, and rode out toward the south."

"Then he's gone to the Purgatoire."

Her voice, when it came again, was filled with fright. "What happened, Black Dog? What went wrong? I was so sure you would return to the village in triumph. I do not understand."

He did not immediately reply. When he did, it was almost as though he was talking to himself. "They were warned. They were ready for us, crouched behind barricades that were too high for horses to jump. I took fifty men into one street with me and only five came out. The rest were butchered and the wounded were killed as though they were dogs."

"But who could have warned them?"

He glanced at her bitterly. "My father warned them. He saw me there and guessed what I meant to do. He warned them and then came here. He didn't even tell me that I would be riding into a trap."

Night Star said timidly: "He meant to tell you before you left. But he fell asleep. He is an old man, Black Dog. He did not mean to sleep but his weariness was too great. When he awoke and found you gone, he tried to overtake you so that he could tell you about the trap."

Julien cursed savagely in English. He lay there, still, but his muscles were tight with strain. His eyes burned as they stared at the teepee top. His voice was scarcely more than a hoarse whisper. "I will kill him. I will stake him out upon the prairie and watch him die. I will laugh when he begs me for mercy."

"No, Black Dog. He is your father."

"He is a betrayer who has caused the deaths of two hundred and fifty Cheyenne warriors."

"He did not mean to let them die. He did not mean to let you go unwarned. I should have wakened him, but I did not know there was reason to. Blame me, Black Dog, because I did not waken him. Kill me, if you must, but do not kill him."

Before he could answer, the teepee flap was flung aside. Standing Moose entered, followed by several of the older men of the village. They did not sit down beside the fire as was customary. They stood in a group, their eyes cold, their expressions harsh with disapproval. "You will leave this village, Black Dog. You are no longer one of us. Take your lodge and your squaw and go far away from here. You have brought defeat to the village and to the Cheyennes. White soldiers will come searching for you. They will kill all The People in this village if you are here. Your medicine is bad and you must go, at once, before the sun sets in the west tonight."

Julien nodded. He stared at the old men bitterly. They had never approved of the things he did. They had never joined him in his war against the whites. They had grudgingly permitted it as long as he was winning and bringing loot to the village because they feared a challenge to their authority if they forbade it. But now. . . .

He said: "I will be gone before the sun sets in the west."

Standing Moose nodded. For an instant there was something close to regret in his eyes. He stared at Julian thoughtfully. "In the old days, you would have been a great war chief, but the old days are no more. The day of the Cheyennes is gone. We will be overrun and our lands taken away from us. The buffalo will disappear. I am an old man who has seen this land before the white men came. I would like to see it that way again but I know it is impossible. The white men have come all the way from the great water in the East. They will not stop their march until they reach the great water in the West. The Cheyennes are finished."

He stared at Julien a moment more. Then he turned and left the lodge.

Julien waited a moment, then followed him. He walked out to the horse herd and caught up three horses of the nine he owned. Riding one, he led the others back.

Night Star had called upon others among the village women to care for the two wounded warriors Julien had brought into his lodge. She was now silently preparing to leave. Julien said: "We will not take the lodge. We will leave everything but what we can take upon our horses and upon our travois."

Night Star nodded silently. Her eyes were downcast, but he could see that there were tears in them. "You are sad that you must leave?"

"I am sad that we must leave."

"You would wish to stay?"

She glanced up at him. "I would only wish to be with you. If I cannot do that, I no longer want to live."

"Nor would I, Night Star."

Julien swung around. Iron Horse stood a few feet behind

him, his wounded arm bound tightly against his body. His face was gray and haggard. He looked as though he might fall at any instant. But his mouth was firm with determination and his eyes showed neither weakness nor indecision.

Iron Horse was the only one left of his original band. Julien's throat felt tight, as did his chest. He said softly: "You are badly wounded, Iron Horse, and the journey ahead of us is long and hard."

The older man's eyes pinched together as though from pain. He said: "If I will slow you down. . . ."

"It is not that, Iron Horse. But you may not live if you go with us."

"It does not matter. I will at least die in the company of a man, not lying in a teepee like a squaw, not among old women who are afraid to fight."

Julien nodded. "Lie down, then, and rest until we are ready. I will get another horse and put a travois behind it. We will travel no slower because of you. We already have one travois that we must take."

Iron Horse went into the lodge, walking steadily though obviously with great effort. Julien went to catch another horse.

The day wore on slowly. Iron Horse slept in the lodge. Night Star worked at packing the travois and the horses. Julien sat before the lodge, brooding, thinking of his father and of what he meant to do to him.

They were ready to go while the sun was yet halfway up the sky. Julien helped Iron Horse to the travois and tied him in. He mounted and led out, trailing the horse behind which Iron Horse rode. Night Star mounted and followed, leading the other horse. The villagers watched them go impassively, neither with regret nor hate.

What lay in the future for him, Julien couldn't guess. Death, he supposed. Alone, with no fierce band of warriors at his back, he would be easily caught, easily taken or killed.

Right now, that didn't seem to matter much. Nothing that happened after he found and killed his father mattered much. But nothing must prevent him from reaching the Purgatoire. He had been cheated of his dream for conquering and driving out the whites. He would not be cheated of this as well. Two hundred and fifty voiceless dead cried out for his success.

XX

Travel was slow for the little caravan. They must, necessarily, travel at a plodding walk, for to go faster would jolt Iron Horse too severely on the travois. The first day they made less than half a dozen miles before darkness forced a halt.

Julien built a small fire in the bottom of a dry wash where its light would not be seen, and Night Star cooked a pot of meat for them.

Julien ate heartily, but Iron Horse ate no more than a few bites, then fell into a deep sleep that was much like death. Julien laid down and also slept, but Night Star remained awake, keeping watch all through the night.

At dawn, they were up and traveling once more, Julien with his eyes intent and bitter, ever resting upon the southern horizon ahead. He spoke little throughout the day, and seemed impatient with the slow pace they were forced to maintain. Night Star watched him constantly when he was not looking, a troubled expression in her eyes. She knew, if he did not, that killing his father would complete his self-destruction, even if he were never caught and hanged for it.

He did not realize it now and would not have admitted it, but Night Star knew he both loved and respected Charles Tremeau. Tremeau had given him his life and had saved it at Sand Creek when he certainly would have died of his wounds.

Perhaps later he would realize that his father had only acted according to the dictates of his conscience, that his father had not intended to let him ride away unwarned. But then it would be too late and the burden of guilt for what he had done would be too heavy to be borne. But she knew she couldn't stop Julien from doing what he meant to do. Nobody could stop him now.

The next day they covered almost twenty miles. The air was warmer. A sheen of new, fresh green covered the plains for as far as the eye could see. Willows in the stream bottoms were loaded with furry gray buds. A few early flowers bloomed.

Julien was cold, almost distant toward Night Star. His face was set, his eyes more bitter than she had ever seen them before. He was worse, even, than he had been upon his return from his first visit to Denver after he had found the bodies of his children in their shallow grave along the Platte.

Her efforts to talk with him failed. So she moved about their camp silently, gathering wood and keeping the fire replenished, moving the horses often so that they could fill their bellies with the new, green grass.

The third day it was another twenty miles. The fourth a like amount. Slowly the distance dwindled between the village of Standing Moose and the ranch on the Purgatoire.

Night Star lost track of time. They crossed the Arkansas and found the mouth of the Purgatoire. They followed its winding course south across the uneven plain. Julien hunted when they needed meat. He kept close watch for enemies, both Indian and white.

The day came, at last, when he halted unexpectedly, turned toward Night Star and Iron Horse, and said: "We are here. This is my father's land."

Night Star felt her chest turn cold. She asked in a soft and timid voice: "How much farther, Black Dog, until we reach his lodge?"

"The rest of today. We will reach his house at dark."

"Do you still mean to kill him, Black Dog?"

"I have not changed."

"And what will happen then? Will not your father's men hunt us down and kill us all?"

"Perhaps. Do you wish to leave me now, while you still can?"

"No, Black Dog. I will stay with you."

The sun slipped down the western sky and set at last behind the distant, haze-shrouded peaks far to the west. In dusk they traveled more slowly and carefully, for they now were very close to their goal.

Julien halted atop a low bluff that looked across the Purgatoire. He sat his horse like a sentinel, staring down.

Night Star moved up beside him. Faintly, in the dusk, she could see the winding ribbon that was the Purgatoire. She could see the cluster of adobe buildings. There were corrals and several small buildings outside the adobe wall that surrounded the house. But no light showed in these.

The house was built in a manner similar to that of the old Bent's Fort, and was surrounded by adobe walls entered through a huge wooden gate. The rooms of the house were built against the walls and connected on the courtyard side by a covered gallery. In the exact center of the courtyard there was a well.

Julien's face was fierce. He turned his horse and rode back from the bluff edge to where the other horses were. He said: "Take Iron Horse now and go. Ride all through the night, straight to the south. I will catch you when I can."

"I would stay with you, Black Dog. Iron Horse would also stay with you."

"Don't be a fool! Do as I say. I cannot escape my father's men if I must worry about Iron Horse and you."

Night Star nodded dumbly. She didn't know if she would ever see him again. He might be killed. But there was nothing she could do. She could not stop him. Nor could she disobey.

She dismounted, picked up the lead rope of the horse drawing the travois loaded with possessions, and tied it to one pole of the travois in which Iron Horse rode. She picked up the lead rope of this horse, then mounted her own. She said softly: "Good bye, Black Dog."

He did not reply. He did not take his eyes from the direction of the house.

Night Star rode slowly away toward the south. She was sure that she would not see him again. He would be killed, if not before he killed his father, then afterward. And even if he was not—where could he go? Where could he find safety from his enemies?

She had gone no more than a mile when suddenly she halted. She looked back at Iron Horse. "I cannot ride away like this. There must be something I can do. . . ."

Iron Horse croaked weakly: "There is nothing."

"You are wrong, Iron Horse. There is one thing." She swung from her horse and swiftly unlashed both travoises. She tied the horses to separate clumps of brush. Then she remounted and cut right at a gallop until she reached the Purgatoire.

It was completely dark. But even in darkness she could follow the river's course. She rode at a reckless run until she saw the adobe walls looming against the sky ahead.

She rode through the gate and into the courtyard. She swung from her horse and ran toward the man suddenly silhouetted in an open door.

It was Charles Tremeau. He opened his arms and she ran into them. Instantly comprehending that she could not be here alone, he kicked the door shut and put his back to it. Looking down into her terror-stricken face, he said: "Julien?"

She nodded.

"And he intends to kill me?"

149

"Yes."

"All right. Stay here." He crossed the room swiftly and blew out the lamps. He returned, opened the door, and slipped silently into the darkness outside. Night Star crouched in a corner and huddled there, waiting for the sound of gunfire outside. There was nothing more that she could do.

Black Dog would hate her for what she had already done, just as terribly as he now hated his father for betraying him to the whites. But perhaps she had saved his life. Even if he hated her, even if he killed her for betraying him.

Julien sat his horse atop the bluff until all vestiges of light had faded from the sky. Stars winked out, shedding a cold, thin light upon the land. In this light, he picked his careful way down off the bluff.

There was fierce anticipation in him that did not reckon with the emptiness that would characterize his life when this act of vengeance was complete. He left the horse while he was yet three hundred yards from the gate and went on afoot.

He moved as silently as a shadow. No twig cracked beneath his moccasined feet. No gravel stirred or grated. He made no more sound than the shadow of a hawk moving across the ground.

He reached the gate and paused, flattened against one side of it. He stared into the courtyard.

The well made a darker shadow in the center of it. Light flickered from two or three of the windows surrounding it. But nothing moved and there was no sound.

He moved slowly, silently, along the covered gallery. His knife was in his hand.

He could not, in spite of himself, stop the memories that this place brought flooding to his mind. His father had owned the ranch for many years even though he had not often lived on it.

150

Julien had come here with his father as a boy.

He remembered the buffalo hide lodge his father had set up sometimes right here in the courtyard because Red Earth Woman could not stand living in a house. Right out here it had stood, with smoke curling up from the smoke flap at its top.

He forced his thoughts away from these nostalgic memories of the past. Red Earth Woman was dead. So was Bird Woman, and Black Feather, and Little Bird. The Plains Indians were dying and a stench of treachery lay across the greening plains. Only death could kill that stench—the death of Charles Tremeau.

He slipped silently ahead, more like a shadow than a man. Once or twice the gleaming blade in his hand caught light from one of the windows or from the stars and reflected it dully. He felt a strange little chill run along his spine. A feeling as though someone were waiting for him—expecting him.

He scoffed at it as impossible. How could anyone possibly know he was coming or that he was here?

He reached the entrance to the main room of the house. He shifted the knife to his left hand momentarily and reached with his right for the knob. There was the slightest scuffing noise on the gallery immediately behind him. He whirled.

Something struck him a glancing blow on the side of the head. He went to his knees and was struck again, this time solidly. The knife was kicked out of his hand before he could bring it into play.

Stunned, numbed, he surged to his feet furiously. He had failed in Denver; he would not fail here. Weaponless, he still would reach his father. He would. . . .

He leaped back, his head beginning slowly to clear. He saw a dark shape facing him, saw others behind that one. He heard his father's voice. "Easy now, boys. No shootin'. I don't want him hurt."

Tremeau spoke then to him. "Come on, hoss. I've shucked my gun. I whopped you with my bare hands when you was growin' up an' I figure I still can. So come on and get it over with."

The combination of these two things—his father's statement that he didn't want him hurt, his father's assurance—only further infuriated Julien. He launched himself at the older man, groping for his throat.

A fist that was like solid rock exploded on the point of his jaw. He stumbled past, even more stunned than before, and fell face down on the gallery floor.

Tremeau's voice penetrated his fading consciousness. "Indians don't use their fists, but white men do. Guess you never learned because you never really wanted to."

Julien came up into a crouch.

Tremeau said: "I tried to catch you an' tell you what I'd done. But you were travelin' too damned fast an' you had better horses than the one I had. Night Star tell you that?"

"She told me." Julien's voice came from between clenched teeth.

Tremeau's voice was suddenly dull, almost lifeless in its tones. "I'm goin' about this wrong, I guess. Beatin' you won't change your mind about killin' me. Man does what he figures he's got to do. Like I did when I warned 'em in Denver that you were goin' to attack. All right. Miguel, toss me that rifle."

Julien heard the slap of hands against a rifle stock.

His father said: "Here. Catch this. It's loaded."

Julien's hands were out automatically and caught the rifle.

Charles said: "All right, damn it. Shoot."

Julien stood frozen with surprise.

Tremeau said: "Miguel, see to it he's allowed to leave, no matter what he does to me. Understand?"

"*Señor*. . . ."

"Damn you, do you understand?" Tremeau roared.

"*Sí, señor.*"

Tremeau spoke to Julien again: "Go ahead then, hoss. Nothin' to stop you now."

Julien flung the rifle to his shoulder. His finger tightened on the trigger. At this range, though he couldn't see his sights, he couldn't miss. There was a scramble behind Tremeau as his men moved to get out of the line of fire.

One little squeeze and his father's treachery would be revenged. One little squeeze. . . .

He could feel his finger tightening. But where was the savage joy he had expected this moment to yield? Had he expected his father to beg?

Sweat popped out on his forehead. The muscles along his forearm were as hard as thong leather. His finger against the trigger was a straining hook.

Suddenly he flung the gun away from him. It landed in the courtyard and discharged with an unexpected roar.

Tremeau's voice was calm, but not surprised. "Can't do it, huh? I didn't think you could."

Julien was shaking violently.

Tremeau said: "The rest of you . . . get out of here."

Julien felt his father's hand upon his arm. He felt empty, drained.

Tremeau said: "Come on inside."

Dazedly he followed his father into the house, somehow not at all surprised to find Night Star there, somehow not angry because she was. Her eyes—no man could ever misinterpret that look in a woman's eyes.

For the first time in many months he faced a future in which there was no war, no violence, no death. Yet he knew that it was an illusion. He would always be hunted like a wolf. He said: "Take care of her. If I live, I will come back someday."

153

Tremeau said: "How many men do you reckon there are that could recognize you in white man's clothes?"

Julien stared at him in surprise. He said: "Two or three."

"And if you went south . . . grew a beard . . . what do you reckon the chances of ever bein' recognized would be?"

A faint smile touched Julien's harsh face. He spoke in English for the first time. "Pretty slim."

Tremeau said: "You talk to your wife. I'm goin' out to get you a wagon an' team and the supplies you'll need. Hunt around and find yourself some clothes."

Julien nodded. He turned his head and stared at Night Star, really seeing her for the first time in many months. She was not Bird Woman and could never take Bird Woman's place. But there could be a place for her that would be all her own. With hate gone, there would be room for other things.

He said: "We will have to use Spanish names. Do you think Iron Horse will stand for that?"

"I do not think he will mind."

"And how will you like being called by another name?"

She ran to him suddenly and threw her arms around his neck. There were tears in her eyes but they were tears of pure happiness. She drew back, her eyes smiling through her tears, and teasing, too. "Will you call your son by that name, too?"

Very gently, Julien held her close to him, as though he would never let her go.

★ ★ ★ ★ ★

GUN THIS MAN DOWN

★ ★ ★ ★ ★

I

Matt Hurst stepped down off the train onto the wooden platform and eyed the town with eyes as bleak as the leaden sky. Snow drove along the ground before the biting January wind, forming tiny dunes as variable as a woman's moods.

He stood for a long moment while his mind digested the unpleasantness of his memories, then he picked up his carpetbag with his left hand, tossed his sacked saddle over his right shoulder, and strode down the slight rise of ground between railroad station and town.

A man's eyes, resting on his home after five years, ought to show something besides this cold unfriendliness. Else why would a man come home? There were a lot of reasons, he reflected, among them a deep need to understand the things that had happened, and a possibility of exacting vengeance.

A few scattered horses lined the town's hitch rails, rumps to the wind, tails whipping between their legs. A lone woman hurried along the street clutching her skirts to keep the wind from lifting them. Smoke rose briefly from half a hundred tin chimneys before the wind snatched it away. And on the far side of town, a school bell clanged for the noon hour.

Hurst looked at the town and cursed.

The hotel, a yellow framed structure with a balcony across the front at the second-story level, seemed to recoil from each new blast of wind, wind that came howling off the rolling sagebrush country to the north of town. Matt shouldered open the door, came into the lobby in a swirling cloud of snow, and dropped his bag and saddle beside the door.

Nothing changes, he thought as he looked around at the game heads hung from the smoky walls, at the worn red lobby carpet, littered as always with cigar ashes and cigarette butts. Nothing changed, not even the sour-faced, bespectacled room clerk, Rudy Littlefield.

Matt stepped across the lobby to the desk and flipped open the register. He signed *Matt Hurst* and looked up at Rudy, a mocking, challenging smile on his lips.

He wasn't a tall man, nor was he overly broad. Unprepossessing because his heavy sheepskin covered and concealed the long, smooth muscles of his shoulders, the deep power of his chest. Unprepossessing until you let your glance dwell on his cold gray eyes, on his mouth so thin and hard and bitter.

Littlefield breathed: "Matt Hurst. I thought you looked familiar. You've growed since I seen you last."

His eyes took on a gleeful excitement. Matt said dryly: "Give me a room and the key to it. Then you can run out and tell the town I'm back."

Rudy eyed the low-slung Colt revolver that peeped from beneath Matt's hip-length sheepskin. He said: "What you goin' to do, Matt?"

"Do? What should I do?"

Rudy flushed and stammered. "Well, you know . . . I mean, you come back to do something about Dan and Will and Frankie, didn't you?"

Matt said: "A room and a key, Rudy."

Let them worry. Let them stew and wonder why he was back. Let them wonder because he was wondering himself. He hated the town and the people in it. He hated the slot they'd shoved him in ever since he was old enough to remember things.

Dell Tillman had always said: "You don't tame a wolf whelp

by treating him good. He's what he is, and sooner or later he'll turn on you."

That was what Matt Hurst was—a wolf whelp. A wolf pup that had run away to keep from being smeared with the same brush that had tarred his father and his brothers. He knew now that he should have stuck.

If he had, maybe things would be different. Maybe Dan and Will and Frankie would still be alive.

Or maybe he should have stayed away. What could possibly be accomplished by returning? One man cannot obtain vengeance against an entire community. And even if he could, would not the very act of obtaining it hurt him more than it hurt the ones against whom he acted?

The carpeting on the steps was a little more frayed than Matt remembered, the hallways a little more dingy. Cooking odors from the hotel kitchen lifted up the stairwell and invariably announced what was being served at the next meal. Today it appeared to be sauerkraut. Matt felt the sudden pangs of hunger.

So immersed was he in his thoughts that he did not notice the girl until he was face to face with her. She stepped to one side to pass, and Matt, stepping aside himself, unwittingly moved the same way and found himself still facing her.

Quickly, embarrassedly he stepped back, and the girl did the same. She laughed, a pleasant, musical laugh, and said: "You stand still. I'll move aside."

Matt flushed, feeling like a fool. "All right," he growled. The girl kept her glance on him with a close interest that further flustered him. And he began to notice her for the first time.

Her hair was like honey in color, having a light yellow sheen on top, deeper, darker highlights beneath. Her skin was smooth and white, her lips full and soft. Her dress seemed unnecessarily tight at waist and bodice, plainly outlining her rather startling figure.

She asked: "You're new in town, aren't you?" He nodded and she said: "I'm Lily Kibben."

"Matt Hurst." The way he said it, the name was a curse.

Lily's eyes widened, and her smile faded. She murmured—"I see."—and stepped quickly past.

He turned and watched her back as she descended the stairs, smiling wryly at her reaction to his name. The wolf whelp is home. That was what all the town would be saying. The wolf whelp is home and there's going to be trouble.

All right, damn it! Trouble hadn't been all that was on his mind when he started back. But if they wanted trouble, then let them have it.

He found his room and opened the door. He strode to the window and looked down into the gloomy street. He saw Rudy Littlefield come out of the Bullshead Saloon across the street and hurry back toward the hotel. He saw Alfred Polk and Dell Tillman come through the heavy winter doors and follow Rudy. Matt moved close to the glass and stared insolently down at them. Rudy glanced up as he approached the hotel, saw Matt, and dropped his glance hastily. Tillman followed the direction of Rudy's glance with his own and scowled when he saw Matt in the window.

Matt grinned. He shucked out of the sheepskin and eased the .45 out of its holster. He spun the cylinder and checked the loads. When he replaced it, he seated it lightly. Maybe they figured on exterminating the Hurst clan once and for all, and he didn't intend to be caught unawares.

He waited in the small room's center, not afraid, but feeling the same tight emptiness in his stomach that fear could engender. He was lonely, really, and angry at himself for being so. And he resented the fact that his homecoming stirred no welcome in a single one of the town's inhabitants. Why? He had never done anything to deserve this. But he was Dan Hurst's

160

son, and because he was, they hated and distrusted him.

He heard Dell Tillman's heavy, arrogant tread on the stairs. It sounded as if Dell was alone. But he knew the sheriff was with Dell and remembered the light way Polk had of walking.

It was Tillman who rapped on the door, loudly, imperatively.

Matt Hurst felt his anger rising. He said shortly: "Come in." And the door banged open. Tillman stepped in first, scowling.

He was a big man, big of body, always appearing larger because of the power he wielded and of which he was so aware. He wore a neatly trimmed beard, and his eyes above it always looked at a man as though he were one of Nature's unpleasant mistakes. He looked at Matt that way now. "Why the hell did you come back?"

Matt stared at him coolly for a moment, trying hard to hold his temper. He said at last: "Damn you, you're in my room. You aren't here because I asked you, either, so keep a civil tongue in your head. I came back because I took a notion to, and maybe because I heard a thing or two."

Alf Polk stepped from behind Tillman, graying, aging, but still with that indefinable quality of confidence and efficiency exuding from him. He said calmly: "Dell, quiet down a mite. Let me talk to Matt."

Dell glared at the sheriff.

Alf muttered: "Matt, Dan and your brothers were killed by a posse acting on my orders. They were caught over in Trout Creek Pass with a herd of DT stock."

"How'd they die?" He thought Dell Tillman's eyes flickered as he asked.

And Alf Polk looked at the floor a moment before he answered. Finally he said with a sigh: "I guess you'll find out anyway. Dan and Frankie were shot. Will was hanged."

Matt felt a surge of passion. "That was on your orders, too, I suppose?"

"No." Alf seemed a little tired suddenly. "No, you know better than that, Matt. I wouldn't order such a thing."

All at once Matt knew that if they didn't get out, and quickly, he wasn't going to be responsible. A lifetime of hatred and resentment seemed to boil abruptly to the surface. He said, his voice even and low-pitched: "Get out of here. Both of you. Get out while you can."

Tillman opened his mouth to bluster, but Alf caught him by the elbow and pushed him around toward the door. His softly breathed words were barely audible to Matt: "Don't be a fool, Dell. Do what he says."

When Tillman was gone, the sheriff turned in the doorway. "Why'd you come back, Matt? You've never done anything that's outside the law. You were doing all right over in Utah." His voice was calm and soothing, a little cautious, too.

Matt flared: "If you don't know, I couldn't tell you. They were all I had. When I got word they had all been killed, I wanted to know how they died. I guess I knew why. But I had to know how."

"Now you know. What you figure on doin' about it?"

Matt's voice was savage, taunting: "Suppose you figure that one out, Sheriff."

Alf Polk shrugged. "Suit yourself, Matt. But be mighty careful. You know how folks react to the name Hurst around here. I'll let you alone until you step out of line. When you do, I'm coming after you."

Matt sneered: "Or send a posse out under your orders . . . with Dell at its head."

Alf looked at him steadily for a long moment. At last he said: "All right. Rub it in. Maybe I deserve it at that." He backed slowly from the room.

Matt Hurst sat down on the edge of the bed and buried his face in his hands. He was shaking with suppressed rage.

Well, he could do the obvious, the thing everybody expected him to do. He could kill Dell Tillman. Then run—and keep on running.

He could carry it further than that. He could find the names of the men who had comprised that posse, and exact vengeance against each one of them. He shook his head. He'd never get that job done. Because Alf would pick him up long before he finished. He could call it a bad job and get out of town.

Or he could go out to the home place and take up where Dan and his brothers had left off.

For some reason, this course appealed to him most. Let Tillman stew a while.

He got up and spilled some of the cold water from the white china pitcher into the graniteware pan. He washed his face and dampened his black, curly hair. He dried on the thin hotel towel and ran a comb through his hair. Then he headed downstairs toward the hotel dining room.

He caught himself thinking of that girl—Lily Kibben—and wondering who she was. She must have come to town after he had left.

Morose, lonely, and very much on the defensive, he came into the dining room and halted in the doorway to eye the thin crowd. Over in the corner sat Dell Tillman and Sheriff Alf Polk. Both of them watched him warily. Nearer to the door sat Lily Kibben, alone. She held her glance on him longer than necessary and, while it was strictly neutral, Matt thought he detected a hesitant invitation in it, too.

On impulse he headed for her table and paused there, looking down, frowning at his own unexpected temerity. He said: "Mind if I join you?" And cursed himself inwardly for laying himself wide open for refusal.

For an instant he thought she would refuse, for into her expression came a definite aloofness. Then she smiled. "Of course not. Sit down."

He released a slow sigh, pulled out a chair, and sat. He found himself grinning at her and said: "I shouldn't have done that."

"Why?"

"Because it would have tickled Tillman to see you refuse."

"But I didn't refuse."

"You were thinking about it, though." This girl was the first one he had encountered here in Granada who looked at him as though he were a person and who seemed able to forget that his name was Hurst.

"Yes. I guess I was. But not for the reason you think. I might have refused any strange man." Her expression was calm and thoughtful, her lips relaxed and pleasant. But her eyes held the faintest shadow of bitterness.

She looked directly at him and said honestly: "Perhaps we're the same kind. You see, I am not particularly well liked in Granada, either."

"Why?" He almost snapped the question.

Her face flushed faintly and she looked away. "I'm not married. I own this hotel, which is a thing no lady should own, and, worse, I run it myself. They place me just a little above the dance-hall girls." She smiled ruefully. "So you see, I can understand your feelings."

Susan Davenport, who had been the hotel's waitress as long as Matt could remember, came up behind her and looked at Matt. "What are you goin' to have, Matt?" Her stance was hostile, her eyes cold.

Matt said: "Sauerkraut's on the menu, isn't it?"

"All right." She went away, her back stiff and straight, with uncompromising disapproval.

Matt grinned for the second time at Lily. "I'm going to have to get used to that."

She looked at him seriously. "Why did you come back? What

can you possibly hope to gain?"

He shrugged. "I don't know. I'll be damned if I do."

He noticed her staring at something over his shoulder, and turned his head. Another girl had come into the dining room, and was striding toward Tillman's table. Lily whispered: "You should remember her. That's Elaine Tillman."

Matt stared, thinking: *Five years makes a lot of difference.* As indeed it did. When Matt had left, Elaine had been a lanky kid in pigtails. There was nothing lanky about her now. Nothing lanky and nothing childish. She pulled out a chair at Tillman's table and sat down. Tillman spoke to her and she turned her head to stare at Matt.

Matt could recall a time when he had been friendly with Elaine, even could remember having a crush on her. But her cool glance revealed nothing of that, for it held only the hostility he was growing so used to.

Yet for some reason, Elaine's hostility angered him inordinately. He stared back at her, deliberately insolent until she flushed and looked away. Tillman half rose from his chair, growling something angrily, but Alf Polk pulled him down again.

And Matt Hurst laughed aloud, mockingly, bitterly.

Lily finished her coffee and stood up, suddenly cool. "I guess I was mistaken about you."

"Why?"

"I thought you might be above that, but it appears that I was wrong." She walked across the room and entered the kitchen.

Susan Davenport brought his dinner, looking oddly relieved. She was an old maid, fiftyish probably and as skinny as an old cow in the spring. She said: "You stay away from Lily, Matt Hurst."

Matt grunted. "She's twenty-one, isn't she?"

Susan slammed his water glass down so hard that water slopped on the table. "You stay away from her. Hear?"

Matt said: "Maybe. Maybe not." He looked across at Tillman, at the sheriff, at Elaine Tillman. He looked up at Susan and thought: *Keep baiting me, all of you. Keep at it. Maybe if you do, you can make me blow up. Then you'll have an excuse to do what you've been wanting to do.*

Susan paled under the concentrated virulence of his glance. She backed away, turned, and fled to the kitchen.

Matt ate hurriedly, hungrily. When he was finished, he tossed $1 onto the table and got to his feet.

He wanted a drink. He wanted a fight. He wanted something that would work this enraged helplessness out of him. But he thought: *You'd better get out of town before you do something crazy.*

He stalked out through the lobby and onto the boardwalk before the hotel. The wind whipped his clothes, penetrating with a cold chill. Snow stung his exposed flesh, as he narrowed his eyes against it. "Tomorrow," he muttered. "Tomorrow I'll ride out home."

Abruptly he crossed the street toward the Bullshead. He banged through the doors and stalked to the bar.

Tillman must have paid his crew today, he thought. There were a full half dozen of them here, drinking at the bar with big, blond Olaf Skjerik, the foreman.

Olaf swung to face Matt, his hand hovering close to his gun. He said harshly: "What the hell did you come back for? You got any ideas of squarin' up for Dan and his thievin' litter? If you have, go right ahead. I'm ready."

He stood, cool and still, his back to the bar. Matt felt his own hand tense, felt the fingers form a claw a scant two inches above his gun grips. He looked at Olaf, at the five DT cowpunchers he'd have to fight, too. He won the battle with himself and said mildly: "With five men backing you, I guess you are ready, Olaf. It takes considerable courage for six men to brace one, doesn't it?"

Arms swinging at his side, he walked over to the bar. He laid a silver dollar down, having first carefully fished it out of his vest pocket. Not looking at Olaf, he took the bottle from the bartender and poured his glass full. He tossed it down and another after it.

Liquor always made him reckless, and he knew this was no time for recklessness. Yet he couldn't seem to control the compulsion that drove him.

Olaf and the DT crew watched him and conversed in low tones. Matt had just finished the forth drink when Dell Tillman banged in, bringing a gust of icy wind and a cloud of swirling snow with him.

He stood at the door with the collar of his Mackinaw turned up about his ears and said harshly: "Olaf, I want to talk to you."

"Sure, boss. Sure." Olaf crossed the room.

Matt turned his back. Tingles of uneasiness ran the length as he listened to the low, indistinguishable murmur of their voices. It took no particular astuteness to guess that they were discussing him.

Abruptly he whirled and walked toward the door. Some perverse obstinacy prevented him from sidling around Tillman's bulky figure, and he jostled the DT owner deliberately.

Tillman showed remarkable restraint, moving aside with only a muttered curse. But Olaf's hand snaked after his gun, coming away only at Tillman's curt: "Olaf! No!"

Matt felt a growing tension within himself. He knew the smart thing would be to get out of town before touchy tempers exploded into violence.

And he might have done this. But standing on the walk before the Bullshead was Elaine Tillman, waiting in shivering silence for her father to reappear.

Matt scowled at her.

She said: "Matt, why did you have to come back? Couldn't

you let well enough alone?" Even with her cheeks red from the cold, she was beautiful. Her eyes were large, deep brown in color. Her hair was jet black, lying in windblown tendrils about her face where it had escaped from the level shawl tied under her small chin.

Matt growled: "You defend shooting Dan and Frankie down? You defend hanging Will?"

"They were rustling, Matt. They were caught with the goods."

"There are courts in Granada County. So far as I know, the penalty for rustling isn't death. It's two years in the state pen."

She shrugged helplessly. "So Dad and Olaf were wrong. Are you going to right that wrong with more killing?"

It was Matt's turn to shrug. He was watching a strange, glowing fire in her eyes. He was watching her mouth turn soft and slack with the thoughts filling her lovely head.

She stepped close to him, and looked up with provocation that may have been entirely unintentional. "Matt, I'm thinking of you."

His mouth twisted. "Sure. Sure you are. I could tell that back in the hotel dining room."

"You're bitter, Matt. Too bitter. You can't spend your life collecting for every wrong that's ever done you."

She swayed against him. And Matt did what any man would do. His arms went around her with the latent hunger of a man who has known few women, who is suddenly offered something by a woman's eyes.

And perversely she regretted the offering instantly as his hands touched her. She struggled.

The saloon door banged open behind Matt. He felt the tug at his belt as his gun was lifted from its holster. And he felt the savage, terrible force of a knee in the small of his back.

He released Elaine and tried to turn. Men were piling out of the Bullshead, but it was Dell who held him. It was Dell who held him with knee at his back and powerful hands on his shoulders while Olaf smashed a giant, hard fist into his unprotected face.

Numb with shock, Matt nevertheless exploded into furious action. He twisted against Dell's grip and the knee slid away. His fist crashed into Dell's face with a chunking noise that left Dell's nose a flattened, bloody mess. Dell turned him loose.

Matt's own straining against the suddenly releasing grip threw him away, threw him across the walk and into the street.

Olaf and his five came lunging after him like a pack of wolves at a fresh kill. And Matt, crouched there in the street, fought desperately and hopelessly for his life.

As Matt came to his feet from that first fall in the street, three simultaneous blows thudded into his body. And all of the hatred he felt for this town and its people came boiling to the surface of his brain. His face twisted, savage, utterly naked in its unmasked passions.

Hatred blazed from his slitted eyes. The wind beat against him, whipped his clothing against his body. He lunged, and an outstretched foot tripped him up. Before he could rise, a kick landed in his ribs, another on the side of his head. Two of the men piled down atop of him and held him pinned to the frozen ground while they beat at him with their fists.

Dimly he heard Tillman's hoarsely shouted order: "Let him up! You can hurt him more that way!"

The two that held him down rolled aside. As Matt stumbled to his knees, he drove himself forward, elbowing one of them in the groin. Matt kicked him viciously as he stepped away.

And they were on him again. Elbows, knees, fists banged into him. A man behind him kicked him in the ankle, and it gave way temporarily. Matt lunged against another of the men, clutching at him for support. And drove his head upward against the man's chin.

It snapped the man's mouth shut and he almost bit his tongue in two. Matt felt the ankle supporting his weight again and shoved the man away from him. He threw a looping left as he did so and felt a wild satisfaction at the solid way it landed.

He heard Tillman's shouting—"Get him! Get him!"—and he thought he heard Elaine's sharp cry.

A hard shoulder drove upward against his jaw, snapping his head back with an audible crack. The landscape and the men closing in whirled before his vision for an instant.

He saw Elaine, wide-eyed with a sort of fascinated horror. There was something primitive in her parted lips, in her hastened breathing, in the hot lights that played in her eyes. But there was no pity in her.

Olaf Skjerik slammed against him then and drove him back against a building wall. Matt twisted, slamming both fists down against the back of Olaf's bowed neck. The man fell like a stunned steer.

He had cut the odds to three to one, and there was solid satisfaction in that. One of those he had downed lay rolling in the frozen street, groaning with pain. Another sat on the edge of the walk, head down, spitting blood between his knees and gagging. Olaf lay utterly still. Matt stepped away from him, nimbly avoiding a rush by two of those remaining. But the third drew his gun and brought it slashing at Matt in a wide, wild swing. The barrel tip grazed his forehead and a flood of gushing blood blinded him. He swiped at his eyes with the back of a numbed hand.

A fist smashed his lip against his teeth. Another rocked his head and blurred his reason. And the gun barrel got him a second time, driving him down into a bottomless pit of darkness.

But not stealing all consciousness or all feeling. Helpless, motionless, he lay on his back in the street while they kicked and beat at him with frustrated and senseless rage.

Until Alf Polk came running across from the hotel, shouting: "Get away from him! All of you!"

It was blessed relief when the hard, raining kicks stopped landing. It was blessed relief to sink away into that bottomless pit where there was no pain but where everlasting hostility hovered in the air like a curse.

II

He was no longer in the street, when his consciousness came back. There was warmth around him, softness under him. His hand moved and felt the rough warmth of a woolen blanket. He opened his eyes and stared upward at the cracked ceiling of his room in the hotel.

He lifted his hand and felt his throbbing face, touching the bandages there. He groaned. Then he saw Alf Polk.

Polk said softly: "Coming out of it, Matt?"

Matt rolled onto his side and groaned again in protest at the pain that shot through his bruised and battered body. It was an effort, but he brought an elbow under him and raised his head and upper body.

His vision cleared and he had the oddest impression of Polk. He thought there was actual pain in the man's face, haunted shame in his eyes. But then it was gone and the sheriff was smiling wryly.

Polk said: "Boy, will you believe me now? Will you go on back to Utah and forget this town?"

Matt shook his head. He flung the blankets back and sat on the edge of the bed, his bare feet resting on the rough board floor. He dropped his head into his hands to ease its throbbing.

In that position he said sourly—"No."—and looked up. "What kind of a man are you, Alf? What hold has Tillman got over you? You let him shoot down Dan and Frankie. Maybe that

171

couldn't be helped. But hanging Will was plain murder and there are laws against murder in every territory in the West. You're sworn to uphold the law. Why the hell don't you do it?"

Polk was silent and his eyes avoided Matt's.

Matt said: "Suppose I was to swear out an assault warrant against Tillman and his crew? Would you serve it?"

Alf got up and walked to the window. He stared down into the street for a long while before he answered. At last he grunted: "Sure, kid. I'd serve it. But don't be a fool. Tillman would have his bunch out in a couple of hours. And you'd only make a laughingstock of yourself."

"Suppose I'd swear out a murder warrant? Would you serve that?"

"I'd have to. But how long do you think you'd last if I did? You'd be the only complaining witness. How long do you think Tillman would let you live?"

"But if he didn't get me?"

Alf sighed. "Tillman would be tried. There'd be no witnesses to appear against him. The men who were along with that posse would deny it. And, Matt, hard as it is to accept, there's a lot of sympathy in any cattle country for a man who catches his own rustlers."

Matt gave him a long, level stare. "Get out of here, Alf. Get out."

Polk walked to the door. His face showed no resentment, but only ill-concealed regret. "All right, kid. I'll go. But I hoped I could talk some sense into you. I hoped you'd see the way the cards are stacked. What are you going to do now?"

"I'm going home. I'll go back out to the old place and live. I'm going to gather up what cattle still carry the Rocking H brand, and pick up where old Dan left off."

"Rustling?"

Matt looked at him pityingly. "Why did I leave this country, Alf?"

"All right. You left because you wouldn't go along with Dan's rustling. But can you ever convince Tillman that you aren't sore enough to misbrand every one of his calves you find? Can you ever convince the people around here that you aren't just like Dan?"

"Tillman will never catch me red-handed. He can't if I let his stock alone."

Alf looked at him a moment more. He said: "You're a fool, Matt. You just haven't growed up yet." He shrugged as he turned away. "Go ahead, Matt. Play out your hand even when you know the deck is stacked. Only don't come crying to me after you've lost your chips." He closed the door behind him.

Matt tried to control the rage that flooded his face with blood. His head pounded. He got up, crossed the room, and peered at himself in the cracked mirror. A bandage was wound around his forehead; another covered a torn ear. Otherwise his cuts had been covered with patches of court plaster.

He was aware of stiffness around his middle and, feeling, discovered a thick tight bandage around his ribs. He wondered how many of them were broken and suddenly understood the sharp pains he'd had whenever he breathed deeply.

He sat back down on the bed, fished makings out of his sheepskin that lay on the floor by the bed, and rolled himself a smoke. He touched a match to its end and inhaled deeply.

All right, he thought, face it. *The world is full of injustice and you've come smack dab up against it. What are you going to do, beat your brains out trying to fight it? Or are you going to act grown up for a change? Act grown up and take the world the way it is instead of trying to change it?*

A man can talk sense to himself but it doesn't always help. Matt's mind was made up as he rose and began to put on his clothes. Gray light filtering into the room told him that dusk was very near.

A knocking at the door startled him, and he looked anxiously for his gun. He found it on the oaken commode and picked it up. It struck him then that the knocking had not sounded like a man's knock would.

Grinning a little sheepishly, he laid the gun back down and called: "Come in!"

The door opened and Lily Kibben stepped into the room. Immediately her face clouded with concern. "You shouldn't be up. You have broken ribs and a concussion." She smiled faintly. "Also you have multiple lacerations, as the doctor put it."

Matt grinned at her. "In everyday language, a sore head."

"Yes." She looked at him with frank interest, a frown of puzzlement on her brow. "Why did you come back? Surely you must have known it would be like this."

"I guess I did. Let's just say I'm mule-headed. Stubborn."

"What are you going to do now?"

"Go out to the home place. Work."

"And try to prove that your father and brothers weren't guilty?"

He shook his head. "No. They were guilty all right. They'd been rustling Tillman's stock for years. I knew it and everybody else knew it, too. I left in the first place because I wouldn't go along with it."

"What do you hope to prove, then?"

He said soberly: "Look. If they'd let me alone today, maybe I'd have turned around and left. It wasn't right that Dan and Frankie were shot, and it certainly wasn't right that Will was hanged. But a man can accept some things, even if they aren't right. Cattle thieves have been hanged before in cattle country. But they couldn't let me alone. As soon as they started pushing, I knew I couldn't leave. Do you see that?"

She said quietly: "Maybe I do see." She studied him for a moment, then said: "I was watching you across the street when the fight started. I saw you try to kiss Elaine Tillman."

Matt flushed; he started to speak and stopped, wondering why it seemed so important that he explain that.

Lily murmured: "Why did you do that? Are you in love with her?"

He shook his head negatively.

"Was it worth what it cost?"

Matt felt his anger stir. He said: "If you were watching, then you know she brought it on. As soon as I touched her, she changed her mind."

Lily crossed the room and stood facing him. She asked again: "Why did you do it?" She watched him, her eyes searching beneath the surface expression of his face.

He frowned. "I don't like to admit this. I thought it was only because she was a woman asking to be kissed, and because I was a man hungry for a woman's kiss. But there was more to it than that. I wanted to show her . . . and show the town . . . that Hurst was as good a name as Tillman."

Lily smiled. She lifted her face and said: "I think I'd like it if you kissed me."

Matt's arms went out and pulled her against him. Her body was warm and soft. Her lips were loose with expectancy, her eyes bright. Matt kissed her.

At first there was only laxness in the girl, limp surrender. He tightened his arms about her, bore down brutally against her lips.

Suddenly her arms went up around his neck. Her body pressed hungrily against him. Her lips moved beneath his. And when she drew away, she was breathing hard. She murmured almost soundlessly: "I think, if I were Elaine, I would regret my struggles."

Matt grinned shakily. "Thanks." He kept his eyes steadily on her, feeling the rise within himself of a hunger that dwarfed any he had ever experienced before.

Lily lowered her glance and backed away. "You must be starved. I'll send you up some food." She turned and walked swiftly through the door.

Matt sat down and pulled on his boots. Oddly, for the first time since his return, he felt proud of himself. He felt as though he were nine feet tall, as though Tillman and the sheriff were his acorn.

He heard the harsh clicking steps of Susan Davenport in the hall, and looked up as she came in with a steaming tray.

She set it down on the table. "*Humpf.* Room service now, is it? What did you do to that girl?"

Matt grinned at her mockingly. "She's twenty-one, isn't she?"

"Some ways. Others, she ain't. You hurt her, Matt Hurst, and I'll. . . ."

"You'll what?"

She faced him defiantly. "I'll kill you myself."

Matt said: "I won't hurt her. Not if I can help it."

Susan flounced out of the room. Matt pulled up a chair and began to eat. He could hear the wind howling outside and he thought of the twenty miles out to Rocking H with dismal dislike. But he knew that if he didn't go out tonight, he'd never go.

So he finished his dinner quickly, gulped the scalding coffee, and slipped into his sheepskin. Then he tramped downstairs and, picking up his saddle and carpetbag, went out into the biting wind.

He gasped as the full fury of the sub-zero blast struck him. And winced at the subsequent pain in his ribs. Bending forward against the force of it, he slogged up the street to the north until he came to the stable.

Behind him the town seemed almost deserted. Here and there

an oil lamp flickered wanly in some window, but the streets were empty, and the horses of Tillman's crew were no longer racked before the Bullshead.

Inside the stable, he dumped his saddle and bag beside the door and went into the tiny tack room that served also as an office for old Si Van Ness. Si sat with his feet against the potbellied stove, and he looked up inquiringly as Matt came in, not recognizing him at first. "Not figgerin' to ride in this, are you, stranger?"

Matt nodded. He fished a bandanna from his pocket, took off his hat, and tied the bandanna over his ears. Si recognized him and slammed his feet down onto the floor. "Matt Hurst!"

"Yeah. Matt Hurst."

"Goin' home?" There was a thinly veiled hostility in Si's voice.

Matt nodded. "I want a horse."

"Dunno. Dunno about that."

"You'd better find out fast. I'll rent him or buy him, but I want a horse."

"Reckon you better buy."

Matt shrugged resignedly. "All right. But no Hurst ever stole a horse and you damned well know it."

"No offense, Matt. No offense."

But the wizened old man didn't back down on his demand that Matt buy the horse. He shuffled into the cold, gloomy rear of the stable and returned shortly leading a big blue roan gelding. Matt carried a lantern out and set it on the floor while he went over the horse. He would not put it past Si to palm off a string-halted or smooth-mouthed horse on him. The horse was sound, however, and young, so he paid the $70 Si demanded without comment.

The town fell behind, and Matt headed directly north along the road. After the first five miles, his feet were numb. He got off and walked a while.

Snow fell thicker now, and began to pile up on the ground.

A sense of hopelessness and depression increased in Matt's consciousness. *Why am I doing this?* he asked himself. It was now obvious that vengeance for the death of his father and brothers was out of the question. It was also obvious that years would be consumed in living down the bad name Hursts had always had hereabouts.

Yet hard as it was, Matt knew it was a thing he had to do if he wanted to live at peace with his own conscience.

Midnight passed. Matt walked enough to keep the circulation up in his legs and feet. He almost missed the turn that led to the Hurst Ranch, but he realized it and retraced his steps. After a few moments, dismounting to walk, he saw the dim hoof prints of horses in the road before him, almost drifted over by driving snow.

Instantly he swung into the saddle, spurred to a reckless gallop. What were they up to now?

He knew, really, even before he saw the glow in the sky. He knew and rode recklessly, his face twisted into a savage, bittern pattern. They had burned him out!

As he rode up before the smoldering ruins, he was shouting at the top of his lungs—shouting curses, blasphemies—shouting threats, and almost sobbing, with hurt and cold and awful frustration.

Chilled and shaking, he piled off the horse and warmed himself in the charred and glowing embers of the house. He looked around at the fire-lit yard. They had burned the barn as well as the house. But the corral stood intact. And dug into a bluff a hundred yards from the house was the spud cellar, something they couldn't burn.

This was the place Matt Hurst remembered from the time he began remembering. It was where he had been born. The buildings stood in the center of a hundred and sixty acre homestead claim. And surrounding that was Rocking H range.

Slumped and somber, he stood and stared at what was left. He was beaten. Even Matt could see that now, and admit it because he had to. It was ride back to town, sell his horse, and get on the train for Utah. A man could stand only so much and Matt had stood it.

Something twitched at his hat, snatched it from his head. The report came instantly, a deep booming report like that of a rifle. Matt hit the ground before its roar had quite died away, lying silent and still.

So he was not even to have his chance to run? Well, to hell with them! He'd not run and he'd not quit. He'd stay, and if death were his due for that, then it couldn't be helped. He'd take a few of them with him.

He made his breathing shallow and waited. After a few moments he heard a soft shuffling in the snow. It came nearer—and then a rifle muzzle dug savagely into his back. He heard a man's hoarse breathing.

Matt suddenly threw himself backward against the rifle muzzle with all the violence he could muster, rolling as he did. He came up grasping the icy gun muzzle in one hand. He pulled it and the rifle-bearer tumbled toward him with a sharp cry. Matt raised his knees and they caught the man in the stomach.

But with the breath that drove so savagely from him the man gasped the words: "Matt! Don't!"

Matt sat up, peering down at the man's shaggy face. "Kip! What the hell are you doing here?"

"Waitin' fer you to come home." Kip struggled to his feet.

"Where were you? I didn't see anyone."

"Sure not. I was in the spud cellar." Kip's voice was cracked and reedy. "Come on. I got a fire goin' in there and it's a sight warmer than it is out here. I got coffee and whiskey, too."

Matt followed him silently across the yard. A lamp was burning in the spud cellar, lighting its moldy walls and dirt floor. There was a moldy, damp smell in the air, but Kip had raked out the disintegrating sacks of rotting potatoes and the floor was as clean as it would ever be.

Kip had made a bunk out of one of the barn doors by laying it on the floor and spreading his blankets over it.

He poured out a cup of coffee, laced it stiffly with whiskey, and handed it to Matt. "You look like you could use this."

Matt asked after the first scalding sip: "Did you see them do this, Kip?"

"I did. Skjerik ramrodded this dirty job. He had three men with him."

"Tillman along?"

Kip shook his head.

"When did they do it?"

"Just after dark." The old man peered at Matt. "What hit you? A freight train?"

Matt made a twisted grin. "Same freight train that burned this place, Kip. Only it was Skjerik and six men."

"What you goin' to do about it?"

Matt shrugged. "I don't know. This is rough on me, but it wasn't for me that I came back. I came back to see if Dan and Frankie and Will got a fair shake. They didn't, but they knew the chances they ran taking Tillman's stock. They got what they knew they would if he caught them."

"You mean to say you don't know?"

"Know what?"

"That they'd quit rustling Tillman's stock. They quit when you pulled out. Dan hadn't changed a brand for damned nigh four years. He wrote a couple hundred letters to different parts of the country, tryin' to find you and get you to come back. I guess he realized you was right."

Matt stared at him, his mouth hanging open. "Kip, you're crazy. Why else would Tillman go after them?"

"He needed Hurst grass. About a year ago he bought the Holt place that borders you on the west. After that, this place cut him plumb in two. He tried to buy it from Dan half a dozen times, only Dan figured maybe you'd want it someday."

A crazy, tight, nervous fury was growing in Matt. "But Alf said. . . ."

"Alf," Kip snorted. "He's been courtin' that daughter of Tillman's. He'd perjure himself to Saint Peter to get her."

"He's twenty years older than her." Matt was incredulous.

"Sure. Them kind want even harder than a young buck. They want so hard nothin' else matters to 'em."

"But how the hell did Tillman get away with it? There's other people in the country. Surely someone knew . . . ?"

"They knew Dan and your brothers were suspected of rustlin'. Dan didn't go around tellin' folks he'd quit. Hursts have had a bad name in these parts for so long, it'd take a sight more than Dan's words to whitewash it anyhow."

Matt whistled. "Kip, how can you be sure?"

"Boy, I was with 'em. 'Twas a blizzard, something like the one tonight. We were movin' a bunch of Rockin' H stuff in to be fed for the winter. They jumped us in that patch of timber over by Oak Springs. We made a run fer it, scatterin' like Dan said. I was lookin' back and seen Olaf and Tillman ridin' together. 'Bout then a low tree limb got me on the side of the head and dumped me out of the saddle. When I come to, I started huntin' around fer Dan and the boys. I found 'em. I found 'em all right. Dan and Frankie shot. Will hanged."

"What'd you do?"

Kip looked at the floor. He cleared his throat. His voice was low and shamed. "Nothin', boy. Nothin'. I knew the thing was so big nobody'd dare let a witness to it live. I knew it was useless to go to Alf Polk. So I just kept my mouth shut. I knew you'd hear about it and come hot-footin' it home. And I figgered I'd be a sight more use to you alive than dead."

"How's it happen they didn't look for you? Didn't they know you were working for the Rocking H?"

"That's just it. I wasn't. Nobody even knew I was in the country. I'd been in Colorado ridin' for an outfit down there durin' the summer. When they laid me off, I drifted in here to see if maybe Dan wouldn't hire me durin' the winter."

Matt realized that his fists were clenched so hard that the nails were biting into his palms. He spat his words out like bullets: "They won't get away with it. They won't get away with it."

III

Matt lay awake most of the night, staring upward into the utter blackness of the cellar. Outside, the wind howled and whined and deposited a six-inch layer of snow on the ground. In the morning, Matt was no nearer a solution than he'd been before.

Essentially Dan's innocence and that of his brothers made no difference at all in the solution to the problem. He was still face to face with the whole country's enmity; he was still confronted with the sheriff's dishonesty and dereliction of duty.

But he remembered the look of shame in Alf Polk's eyes and his words: *All right. Rub it in. Maybe I deserve it at that.*

He made up his mind and rolled out of his blankets. As he did, Kip stirred and sat up sleepily. Matt built a fire in the cast-iron stove Kip had apparently salvaged from the ranch junk heap. Kip got a quarter of venison where he had hung it outside and cut off a half dozen steaks. He mixed up some biscuits and slid them into the oven.

"Matt, you look like mebbe you've made up your mind."

Matt nodded. "I'm going to take a whirl at Alf Polk. He wasn't along on that raid when Dan and the boys were killed.

Maybe he doesn't know it was a put-up job."

"What if you're wrong?"

"I won't be any worse off than I am right now. They're doing their damnedest to get me anyway."

Kip's seamed, aged face showed his disapproval. But he only grunted. He crossed the room, got his rifle, and began to clean it. He said: "I'll get ready, son. They'll be after me quick as Alf can get in touch with Tillman."

Matt said: "Kip, it's our only chance. Some of the men who were along on that deal are bound to've read the brands on that bunch of stuff. They'll know they weren't DT stock but our own. Get 'em in a jail cell, and I'll lay you ten to one they'll talk."

Kip shrugged. "Wish I had your confidence. Well, hell, I'm old anyhow. I got to go sometime, and I'd rather go with a bullet in me than lay in a bed and die slow."

Matt grinned as he mopped gravy from his plate with a broken biscuit. "Worrying is what gave you all that gray hair."

He got up and shrugged into his sheepskin. Outside, the world was dazzling with bright sunlight on fresh snow. The sky was as blue as Lily Kibben's eyes. He got his horse from the corral where he had put him last night late and saddled up, wishing the animal had had some hay last night, or at least some grain. But the haystack had caught from the barn, and even yet was smoldering, sending a column of blue smoke into the sky like a signal. All the grain had been in the barn. He made a mental note to have a load of hay and grain sent out today from town.

Kip looked up at him after he had mounted. He said: "Let's see. It'll take you till ten or eleven to get to town. It'll take Alf till two to ride out to Tillman's. So I reckon we can expect company along about three or four. You be back by then?"

"Sure."

"Bring me back boxes of Forty-Four-Forties. Better bring a couple of boxes of Forty-Fives for yourself. We'll likely need 'em."

Matt snorted and rode away.

Riding, he considered Kip's doubt, weighing it against his own confidence. All depended, he was aware, upon Alf Polk's honesty. If he were mistaken in giving Alf credit for honesty, then Kip was right. They'd fight to the death right in the spud cellar.

But if Alf were honest, he'd take a posse out to DT for Tillman, Olaf Skjerik, and the men who had ridden on that murderous errand.

The air warmed rapidly under the bright sun as Matt rode. Underfoot the snow turned soft, and it was melting away from the high spots that were all but scoured clean.

Matt's mind was filled with memories of his father and two brothers and with regrets that none of Dan's many letters had found him. He would have liked to have made his peace with them before they died. He would have liked to unsay some of the harsh things he had said on the day he left.

He was touched by the fact that Dan and his brothers had given up their raids on DT stock because of his leaving. And he was more than ever determined to see that their murderers came to justice.

Engrossed by his thoughts, he did not see the rider who pulled out of a side road and stopped to wait for him until he was almost upon her.

It was Elaine Tillman. Her smile was bright as if a trifle uncertain.

He stared at her, unsmiling.

She faltered: "Matt, I'm so awfully sorry about yesterday. But I don't think I could have stopped them."

"You didn't even try. And you know damned well you were

asking me to kiss you."

"Matt, you're wrong. I can see how you might have got that idea, but. . . ."

Matt laughed harshly.

Elaine flushed. She said defiantly: "All right. I was asking for it. But as soon as you touched me, I remembered Dad and Olaf inside the saloon. I knew they might come out at any minute. I was afraid of what they'd do if they found me in your arms. So I struggled, hoping to get loose before they came out. You mustn't blame them too much, Matt. Your father and brother stole a lot of Dad's cattle. They naturally hate the name Hurst."

Matt's expression didn't change. His eyes were bullet-cold. "Did you know they burned me out last night? House, barn, haystacks. I spent the night in the spud cellar."

Elaine showed surprise that could not have been feigned. "Matt, it couldn't have been them. Dad wouldn't do such a thing."

Again Matt laughed. "They were seen. And I'll tell you something else. Dan and Frankie and Will were driving a herd of Rocking H stuff when they were killed. It was deliberate, cold-blooded murder. They hadn't stolen a DT critter for four years . . . not since I pulled out of the country. And Dell Tillman knew it."

Elaine's eyes blazed. "Matt Hurst, you're a liar."

He shook his head. "I've got proof of it."

"Proof. Proof. What proof could you have?"

He smiled coldly. "An eyewitness."

"Who?"

"Same one that saw them burn the buildings at Rocking H last night. Kip Reynolds."

She pulled up her horse and stared at him. She must have read truth and sincerity in his eyes, for she suddenly slumped in the saddle and the fight went out of her.

"What are you going to do?"

"I'm going to see Tillman and Skjerik dangling at the end of a rope. I'm going to see every man that was with them that night rotting in the state pen. I'm going to see Alf Polk driven out of the country, disgraced because he permitted it to go unpunished. And I'm going to see the name of Hurst respected and that of Tillman dirtied the way my own name has been dirtied."

"Is that all you want, Matt?"

"Not altogether. I want the buildings at Rocking H paid for."

Suddenly Elaine slipped out of the saddle. She walked up to the side of Matt's horse and stood looking up at him. Tears of humiliation stood out in her eyes. She fumbled in the pocket of her wolf-skin coat, but Matt paid little attention to that. He thought she was searching for a handkerchief.

She said: "Matt, please. I've had no hand in all these things. Must I suffer, too?" Her hand came out of her pocket and she caught at Matt's cinch as the horse side-stepped nervously away. She was pleading: "Matt, you used to like me. And I liked you, Matt, only I was afraid of Dad."

Matt felt a moment's doubt. Then his mind pictured Will, swinging in the icy breeze because Tillman was greedy, pictured Dan and Frankie, still on the ground while snow drifted over their unfeeling faces—because Tillman was greedy.

She said quickly: "Matt, is it all dead, your feeling for me? Because if it isn't, we can still be happy." She made a shaky smile, and in her eyes was promise, invitation. "Get down, Matt. Please."

Matt's eyes searched her face. Odd, the resemblance it bore to her father's even while it was entirely different. Odd, that resemblance—the same arrogance, carefully masked, the same unbending ruthlessness. Dell would do anything to attain his ends, and Matt knew suddenly that Elaine would, too.

He wanted to laugh, to mock her offer. But his innate sense of chivalry would not permit it. He said gently: "It's too late, Elaine. Too many things have happened. I couldn't let Dell get away with those three murders even if I wanted to."

Now her carefully masked arrogance and ruthlessness showed in her face. Her expression contorted with balked, frustrated fury.

Matt's horse suddenly shied away from the girl. Matt felt his saddle turn and felt himself dumped onto the snowy ground. Elaine stood ten feet away, looking at him, a cryptic smile on her face, a small pocket knife in her hand.

Matt struggled to his feet, more surprised than angered. "What the hell did you do that for?"

She laughed softly, mockingly, and her eyes held a gleam of triumph. "You're beaten Matt Hurst. Do you know what I'm going to do?"

He shook his head, thoroughly puzzled.

She put the knife in her pocket, and her hand came out holding a Derringer, which she pointed steadily at him. "I'm going to tear my clothes and scratch my face. I'm going to ride into town and say that you attacked me." Her free hand went to her face and her nails raked deliberate gashes across her cheek. Matt tensed, started toward her, but a freezing of her glance, a tightening of her hand around the grip of the gun halted him.

She said: "Matt, don't do it, or I'll kill you."

"You wouldn't get away with it." But he knew he was wrong. She would get away with it. The word of a Tillman was better than that of a Hurst any day. He stopped, holding his hands rigidly at his sides while he watched the mounting hysteria in Elaine.

She caught the neck of her coat and ripped it open, and the buttons popped off onto the snowy ground. She caught at her bodice and ripped it downward, exposing to his startled eyes a smoothly rounded, swelling white breast.

Again Matt tensed, wanting desperately to halt this. There was something indecent about it that shocked him. Yet what could he do? Even if he escaped being shot by that steady gun in her hand, what would have been accomplished? He could not restrain her indefinitely. He could not hold her here all day.

He whispered: "Elaine, stop it. This is crazy."

"Is it? I don't think so. I think it's the only way I can beat you, Matt."

Her hand went upward to her hair, deliberately began pulling the hairpins and dropping them. Her hair streamed in a cascade about her shoulders.

And Matt knew an empty, defeated feeling. She was right. He was helpless to stop her and he was beaten. He'd had Tillman right where he wanted him; he'd been able to foresee justice done for the murder of his father and brothers. Now, all hope of that was gone.

The townspeople would believe Elaine. Nothing would suit them better than to believe that this final degradation was possible for a Hurst.

Still holding the tiny gun on him, Elaine walked over and mounted her horse. She rode away, unspeaking but smiling triumphantly.

With violent trembling fingers, Matt got out his pocket knife and walked over to where his saddle lay. He began to mend his cinch.

His emotions ran the gamut, in the next few moments, from utter despair to towering rage. He cut holes in each end of the cut cinch latigo, then cut off one end of his leather saddle strings, and with this laced the two ends together.

He caught his horse and slammed the saddle up with un- necessary viciousness. The horse shied and looked at him with reproachful eyes. Matt leaped into the saddle, but he did not dig in his spurs. Instead, he looked toward town, looked back toward Rocking H, and then looked in the direction of Tillman's DT.

An idea began to blossom in his head, giving hope to his reluctance to run.

When he did finally sink his spurs, his horse was headed for Tillman's place. He was through running. If he ran now, he knew what the end would be. They'd hunt him down on Elaine Tillman's testimony until they found him. And they'd find him if it took ten years. When they did, there could be no end but the hangman's noose. Not even a trial to precede it. For only this way could the men of the frontier keep their women safe from the riff-raff that prowled its lonely reaches.

Matt's horse pounded away the few short miles that lay between the place that Elaine had left him and the Tillman Ranch. A little before eight he topped a rise and looked down into its yard. He knew the next few minutes would draw heavily on his dwindling patience. So he steeled himself to wait.

Apparently breakfast had been over for some time. Yet the crew was still in the bunkhouse, receiving instructions on the day's tasks. Matt saw Tillman come out onto the long verandah of the house, pause, and light a cigar.

Hatred poured through Matt like a poison. His hands trembled and his face went white. It took all of his self-control to keep his hand off the grips of his gun, even though he knew this was an impossible range for a revolver.

Tillman puffed luxuriously for a few moments, then strolled ponderously toward the bunkhouse. He met Olaf at the door, and the crew spilled out around the two as they stood talking.

There was a brief commotion in the corral as each roped out a horse for the day. Then the crew mounted, split, and in two bunches rode at a slow trot away from the ranch, leaving Tillman and Skjerik in the bunkhouse doorway.

The sound of their talk carried clearly in the crisp air if the words did not. Matt began to curse softly, virulently under his breath. "Separate, damn you. Separate. I can't jump you both and I've got to have Tillman."

As though in immediate recognition of his command, Olaf slouched away toward the corral. And moments later rode out on the trail of one of the crews.

Matt did not move. Tillman watched Olaf until he was out of sight. Then he turned and made his way toward the house.

Matt wasted no time at all now. At a run, he caught his horse and swung himself to the saddle. He urged the horse into a swift, relatively silent running walk and headed off the rise toward the ranch yard, hoping that Tillman would not pause at the window and look out.

He reached the yard without incident. Still it was touchy, for one of the crew might return after something forgotten in the morning's haste.

He tied his horse to the porch rail and, walking soundlessly, mounted the steps. Since the morning was fairly warm, Tillman had left the door ajar. Matt took an instant to draw his gun and thumb back the hammer and then he stepped into the house.

The huge front room was empty. Matt tried to recall from the couple of times he had been in this house where the office was exactly. He decided it was off the oak-paneled dining room.

He saw that he had been right an instant before he stepped into the office doorway, the gun steady in his hand.

Dell Tillman looked up with surprised annoyance that changed in a miraculously short instant of pure, undistilled rage. He said: "Get out of here."

Matt's lips curled unpleasantly. "Not until you come with me."

"Are you crazy? Have you gone plumb nuts?" Tillman's hand

yanked open one of the desk drawers before him and dived inside.

But Matt was quicker. With two swift strides he reached the desk and, leaning over it, slashed savagely at Tillman's face. The gun barrel caught Tillman's nose, broke the cartilage in it, and shoved it to one side, bleeding internally and purpling outside.

Tillman forgot the gun in the drawer. He clapped a hand to his nose, and tears of pain stood out in his eyes and rolled across his cheeks. But he uttered no sound.

His eyes were blazing coals as they stared their defiance at Matt.

Matt said evenly: "You're coming with me."

Matt's gun barrel slashed again. This time it caught Tillman on the side of his jaw. The sound of bone breaking was plain in the room. And this time, a howl of pain, almost a sob, came from Tillman's tightly held lips. Now on the floor, his other hand went up and shoved his sagging jaw back into place. Pain whitened his face and brought beads of sweat out on his broad forehead.

Matt said evenly, hiding the sickness that seared his soul: "Get on your feet and come with me. Or do you want another taste of this?"

Tillman cringed. He got up and came around the desk, still holding his shattered jaw carefully in one hand. He said weakly: "Let me tie this up. Man, I've got to have a doctor."

"Later." Matt laughed sourly. "I want it to hurt you till we get where we're going. I want it to hurt you bad. Maybe if it hurts you enough, you'll want to talk. Maybe you'll want to tell me everything you know without making me hit you again."

He herded Tillman ahead of him out the door. Tillman winced as the cold air touched the exposed roots of his broken teeth. Matt crossed the yard and, watching Tillman out of the corner of his eyes, roped a horse out of the corral. He pulled a saddle from the top rail and cinched it down on the horse's back. He walked across the yard, mounted, and returned.

"Get up," he said curtly. "And don't forget. There's nothing but death in this for me if I get caught. If we run into someone, I'm going to kill you first. With a shot right in the belly where it'll hurt before it kills you."

Tillman mounted painfully. And Matt headed out at a trot.

A trot is the most painful gait imaginable for a man in pain anyway. With Tillman's broken and sagging jaw, it was torture. Whenever Tillman would pale and sway in the saddle, Matt would slow to a walk. And when Tillman would apparently recover, he'd again urge the horses into that bone-jolting trot.

Twice Tillman tried to speak, but Matt only said brutally: "Shut up!"

Just before noon, they reached the dug-out spud cellar on Rocking H. Kip came out of the cellar door and stood, rifle in hand, watching. Matt said harshly to Tillman: "Get down!"

Tillman slid off his horse, nearly collapsing as his feet touched the ground. Matt dropped his horse's reins. He shoved Tillman ahead of him to the dug-out door.

Kip's eyes widened. "What'd you do to him?"

"It's a long story that I'll tell you later. Something came up that made me change my plans this morning. Go look in my bag. You'll find a paper and pencil. Bring it out. I want to write down what Tillman's got to say."

Tillman showed no resistance, indicated no will to refuse.

Kip came back with a pad and pencil and Matt sat down with his back to the door. On the top of the sheet he wrote *Statement* and the date, *January 27, 1887.*

He looked up at Tillman. "Make it easy on yourself. What happened the day you jumped Dan and my two brothers."

Tillman hesitated.

Matt said: "Kip, hit him in the jaw with your fist."

192

Kip started toward Tillman. But Tillman said: "No. I'll tell you."

"Go ahead." Matt poised the pencil and began to write swiftly as Tillman talked.

"I rode in that morning and told Alf that Dan was moving a herd of DT stock. Alf deputized me and Olaf, and we took Sam Willis, Joe Furness, and Utah Dunning."

"Five of you, then."

Tillman nodded. "We caught them over by Oak Springs."

"Did they have any DT stock?"

Tillman shook his head after a wary glance at Kip. "Only Rocking H stuff. We jumped them and shot two of them down. We caught Will and strung him up."

"Did your crew get a look at the cattle?"

Tillman shook his head. "It was snowing. Nobody was payin' any attention to the cattle, and they scattered anyhow. But Joe Furness's horse was shot out from under him, and, while he was lying there, a little bunch of the cattle went past him. He asked Olaf about it later. Olaf told him he'd kill him if he opened his mouth about it."

Matt began to grin. He looked up at Kip. "We've got two eyewitnesses then."

Tillman looked surprised.

Matt said: "There was a fourth man along with them that day. Kip here. He'd just drifted in from Colorado and Dan agreed to give him his keep for his winter's work." He got up and handed the pad to Tillman. "Sign it."

Tillman did. Matt folded up the paper and handed it to Kip. "Keep this. When the sheriff arrives, pay no mind to what he's got to say about me. But make him read this."

Kip grinned. "All right."

But Matt did not return the grin. He said soberly: "You haven't heard the worst of it yet. I'm supposed to have attacked

Elaine Tillman. If I can talk my way out of that one, I'll be better than I think I am."

Tillman's face grew slowly purple.

Matt said: "Do you know what your daughter did? She cut my cinch this morning so I couldn't beat her to town. She clawed her own face and half tore her clothes off. Then she took out for town."

Tillman lunged at him. "Liar!"

Kip tripped the man. But his eyes were cold as he looked at Matt. "I hope he's wrong, Matt. I got no use for a man that'll force a woman."

Matt grinned sourly: "Even you huh, Kip?" He mounted and rode away, fuming.

Halfway to town, Matt topped a low rise of ground over which the road ran and saw the sheriff's posse sweeping toward him. He was about to leave the road and seek concealment when the sheriff led his men off the road, taking the more direct route across country toward Rocking H.

Matt, mostly concealed by the rise, sat looking ruefully after them. A man wouldn't have a chance with a bunch like that. He wouldn't even get back to town. They'd hunt around until they found a cottonwood limb strong enough to hold him, and then they'd hang him.

Shrugging, he lifted the blue roan to a mile-eating, rolling lope, and stayed with the gait steadily all the way to the outskirts of Granada. There, he left the horse in an abandoned, sagging building and proceeded on foot.

He walked openly down the street toward the center of town, nervous and very much alert, ready at an instant's notice to snake his gun from its holster and start blasting away. He didn't intend to be taken alive, to be hanged for a crime of which he was wholly innocent.

The very unexpectedness of his presence here must have carried him through, for he reached the alley behind the hotel without incident, save for a searching stare given him by an oldster who came out of the Chinese restaurant next door to dump a pan of dishwater.

He went on past the hotel, waiting until this oldster should go back inside the restaurant. When he did, Matt whirled and ran back to the rear door of the hotel. He entered, closed the door behind him, and stood, back to the wall, waiting for his eyes to become accustomed to this dimness after the sun glare on new snow outside.

He stood in a storeroom, piled high with canned goods, barrels of sugar, molasses, and crackers.

There were two doors leading out. One, Matt surmised, led to the kitchen, and he guessed that the one that showed the most wear was probably the kitchen door. He crossed the room and opened the other one.

Cautiously he peered through. He was looking into a long hallway, which ended in the lobby thirty feet away.

He slipped through the door and closed it behind him. He advanced along the hallway until he could look into the lobby. Now, he realized, he needed some luck. Somehow, he had to find Lily Kibben without being seen himself.

The lobby was deserted, save for the clerk poring over a ledger at the desk. It was midafternoon, and Matt knew the dining room would also be deserted. The chances were good that Lily was in her room on the second floor.

He made the stairway without being seen and crept silently upward. He reached the top and paused, trying to remember the direction Lily had been coming from when he'd met her that first day.

He had a vague memory of her coming from around to the left of the stairway—and there were only two rooms there.

He knocked softly on the first one, numbered *203*. He got no answer, so he moved on to the second, *205*. He heard steps inside the room, and grew tense as he waited.

When Lily opened the door, he released a long sigh of relief.

Her face, when she saw him, seemed to smooth out into cautious neutrality. "What are you doing here? Don't you know how dangerous it . . . ?"

"I know." He shoved past her and closed the door. "First of all, do you believe I attacked Elaine?" he asked levelly.

"Did you?"

"No. I didn't."

"Then who did?" Her eyes withheld judgment.

"Nobody." He crossed the room and sat down tiredly on the bed. He looked around him. Lily's room was a feminine room, from frilly lace curtains at the window to the satin spread on which he sat. A feminine room that had a light fragrance of woman and woman's perfume.

"I don't understand."

"I met her on the road this morning. I told her I had proof that my father and brothers had been driving their own stock the day they were jumped by Tillman. I told her I was going to the sheriff with the proof."

"What was the proof?"

"An eyewitness Tillman didn't know existed. An old-timer that's been around Rocking H off and on for years. He told me Dan hadn't misbranded a steer since I left four years ago. He told me Tillman wanted Rocking H and that was why he rigged up that rustling scheme."

"Then what happened?"

"When Elaine became convinced that I was telling the truth, she started to plead with me." Matt felt a flush stealing into his face. He said: "She came over to my horse and grabbed hold of the cinch. First thing I knew, I was on the ground, and my saddle was, too. She'd cut the latigo. She pulled a gun on me, said she'd shoot if I tried to stop her. She clawed her face, ripped her clothes, and took down her hair. She told me I'd best get out of the country because she was going into Granada and tell that I'd attacked her."

For the first time, Lily's expression showed belief. "What did you do?"

"What could I do? I could have made a try for her gun, and maybe I'd have got it. But that wouldn't have helped. I couldn't hold her there forever. I figured I was cooked. But I wasn't going to let her stunt get Tillman out of paying for killing Dan and my brothers. So I rode over to DT and kidnapped him. I beat him up some with my gun barrel. I took him over to Rocking H and made him confess in front of Kip Reynolds."

"Matt, Matt, what are you going to do now? They'll lynch you if they can catch you."

"I know it." He got up and faced her, standing close. "I just wanted you to know the truth from me. I didn't want you thinking that what Elaine said was true."

If he had needed a reward for the risks he had taken coming here, he got it now. He found it in the shining brightness of Lily's eyes. "Thank you, Matt."

He turned toward the door.

Lily asked: "What are you going to do?"

He shrugged. "Run, I guess. I don't see how I can save myself. But at least, Tillman and Olaf Skjerik will pay for what they did. I only wish there wasn't so damned much snow on the ground. I won't have much chance. . . ."

Lily interrupted excitedly: "Matt, wait. Did you struggle at all with Elaine this morning?"

"I never touched her."

"Matt, are you sure? It's important. Are you sure you never touched her?"

He nodded, puzzled. Flushed, excited, Lily began to talk. As she did, a flicker of hope began to glow in Matt's eyes. Ten minutes later, he slipped swiftly down the stairs, back to the alley by the same route he had followed coming in.

There was no difference in the way he walked when he came to the street. Before, he had come with his head averted, with his hat pulled low over his eyes. Now, he strolled along boldly, looking each man he met straight in the eyes.

The third one recognized him. Matt saw the man's face pale, saw his mouth drop open. He went on past, and felt the man's eyes boring into his back. He waited another instant, and then he stole a quick look behind him. The man was running frantically along the street toward the center of town.

When he was out of effective pistol range, the man began to yell: "It's Hurst! Matt Hurst! He's right here in town, bold as brass. The damned skunk!"

Matt smiled faintly. He continued to walk unhurriedly. A rifle boomed out behind him and the bullet tore splinters from the frame building wall beside him.

Feigning surprise, Matt looked around. He could see them coming, a ragged line of them, like skirmishers in an Indian battle. As they came, order began to emerge from their confusion. Matt heard the authoritative voice of Judge Fisher, saw his tall, spare figure in the vanguard of the approaching mob.

Matt broke into a hard run.

He went around a corner, running as hard as he could. In seconds, a few of that mob would be mounted. They'd run down a man afoot in no time.

He reached his horse. He heard the howl of the mob plainly and knew they were drawing close, too close. He heard the pound of hoof beats.

He mounted and spurred his horse savagely out the door and into the open, ducking low to avoid the door frame. And went out of town at a hard run with his mounted pursuers only a short hundred feet behind.

For the first two miles, Matt rode as hard as he could, and barely managed to stay out of range of their booming guns. But at last, they apparently decided to wait for the remainder of the mob to catch up, and so slowed to a walk. They had seen the plain trail he made in the snow and had known he could not get away. Matt put about a mile between himself and his pursuers, and then slowed his horse as well. The animal was breathing hard, was sweating heavily. And he was tired. Hardly in condition to serve a man who had to escape.

At a walk, then, Matt left the road and pointed the horse toward Rocking H. But as he rode, he began to doubt the wisdom of Lily's suggestion. He began to doubt, and loosened the bandanna around his throat instinctively as he thought of the rope they would put around his neck.

Clouds had drifted across the sun, black, lowering clouds that forecast another storm. Matt tipped up his face and tried to estimate how long it would hold off before it struck. Four or five hours, he hoped. Four or five hours.

Always behind him were the angry ones, the ones who wanted his blood. A couple of miles short of Rocking H another group pounded up to join the first. Immediately they all surged forward at a hard run.

Matt shrugged and touched the roan with his spurs. Rested a little, the animal answered with a burst of speed. And at last, Matt rode in sight of the Rocking H.

The yard was jammed with the horses of the sheriff's posse. There was a cluster of men before the dug-out cellar. Matt saw Tillman sitting dejectedly on a box. A white bandage around his jaw, tied up on top of his head, made him stand out plainly.

Matt galloped into the yard, yelling: "Here I am, Sheriff! Come and get me." And pounded out away from it before they recovered from their surprise enough to reach for their guns.

Immediately after leaving, Matt slowed the roan a little. He knew they'd be milling around in the yard for a while before they got organized. Grimly he realized that when they did, there would be over fifty of them on his trail.

He reached the place where the lane to DT joined the road well ahead of them. He dismounted, concealed his horse in a dry wash, and with his rifle poked up out of that same wash, settled himself to wait.

IV

Lily had barely reached the street when she heard the cry lifted: "There he goes! Get him, damn it, get him!"

Immediately, almost, from the doors along the street, men ran out, carrying rifles, revolvers, pitchforks. They formed a ragged line across the width of the street, grim-faced men who advanced toward the edge of town with purposeful determination.

There was something cold about them all that struck terror to Lily's heart. They would be merciless when they caught Matt. For in the minds of all he was convicted, guilty. The word of a woman, particularly a woman such as Elaine Tillman, could not be doubted.

Judge Fisher took charge, shouting crisp, concise orders. He sent half a dozen men to the livery stable after horses. He instructed those others who had horses saddled to get them immediately and try to head Matt off.

And less than two minutes later, six horsemen swept out of town, a short forty yards behind the fleeing Matt Hurst.

Lily felt a cold touch of fear in her spine. She knew abruptly that if her plan failed, then Matt Hurst's blood would be on her hands.

She was thinking, too, that the sheriff was in love with Elaine, thinking that he would not be inclined to believe Matt's story that Elaine had deliberately lied about his attacking her. She was aware as well that Matt, knowing his own innocence, would rely too much on his ability to convince others of it.

Yet she knew the men of this country. And she knew that not one of them would consent to a hanging if a woman were present.

She broke abruptly away from the hotel verandah and, lifting her skirts, ran swiftly as she could toward the stable. Si Van Ness firmly and stubbornly refused to catch and saddle her horse until all of the men waiting were mounted and gone. Lily was forced to wait helplessly, fuming.

At last her horse was ready and, although she was wearing a full-length skirt, Lily mounted astride. She was not much of a rider, and her horse was old and patient. Lily had no spurs, but a small quirt that she had never used hung from her saddle horn. She took it down and belabored the old horse's rump until he lifted resentfully into a half-hearted trot.

The miles dropped behind with agonizing slowness. Tears of helpless frustration welled up into Lily's blue eyes and ran across her cheeks unheeded. *Oh, God,* she prayed. *Let me get there in time. Let me get there in time.*

She thought of the short time she had known Matt Hurst, and of how much he had come to mean to her. She knew that in Matt was a great capacity for living, for laughing and loving.

She wondered if his feelings toward her were the same as hers toward him. Perhaps he had only felt a normal man's hunger for a woman, and perhaps that explained his taking her in his arms, his kissing her.

The thought depressed her, and again she began to quirt her horse. She had to beat them to Matt. She had to.

She almost passed the turn-off that went into Tillman's place, but reined in abruptly and whirled around as a call came to her from a dry wash off from the road.

"Lily! Turn that horse around and get back into town. They'll be here any minute."

Lily started to protest, but hardly had she uttered a half dozen words when she heard the confused, distant shout of the posse.

She heard Matt's urgent shout. "Distract them for just a minute! Stop them here at the forks. Then you get back into town!"

She had no time to answer that, for they were upon her, pulling their plunging horses to a sliding halt. Lily raised her hand.

The sheriff scowled at her and growled irritably: "What are you doing away out here, Miss Kibben? Don't you know Matt Hurst is somewheres around?" He turned to his posse. "Samuels, ride into town with her. See she gets there safe."

For an instant there was silence. It was broken by Matt's cold, clipped voice from the draw: "Don't a damned one of you stir a hair. I've got a rifle here and I'll use it, make no mistake about that."

Someone in the group stirred, and the rifle barked.

Matt said sharply: "Think I'm fooling? The next bullet will kill someone."

The sheriff growled: "Careful boys. Do what he says. Any man that would. . . ."

Matt snarled: "Shut up."

Judge Fisher asked: "What's the idea, Hurst? What do you want?"

"I want you to look at something. You and the sheriff. The rest of you stay put."

Fisher shrugged wearily. "I suppose you want us to believe you never touched Miss Tillman."

"Exactly that. Lily, take the sheriff and the judge and circle around to Tillman's lane. Pick up Elaine's tracks in the snow and follow them here to the main road."

"What'll that prove?"

Matt said: "It will prove that I was never closer than ten feet to Elaine except at the time she cut my cinch latigo. You'll find her hairpins and buttons from her coat lying there at the fork and not a damned track but hers anywhere around." Matt permitted himself a faint, sour grin. "I'm a slick article, Judge, but not slick enough to attack a woman without my tracks mixing with hers. Go on, take a look."

Judge Fisher reined his horse over and crossed to the Tillman lane. With his eyes on the ground, with the sheriff and Lily following him, he traced Elaine's tracks to the main road, careful not to cross or foul any of them with his own.

When he looked up, he said: "Elaine Tillman lied. Tracks say Matt's telling the truth."

There was a sudden, swelling murmur from the packed group of men.

The judge yelled: "All right! Any of you that want to, come over here and look for yourselves. Careful, though, I don't want these tracks messed up."

A man in the crowd said plaintively: "Now why in hell would a woman do a thing like that?"

And the sheriff replied, his voice faint and weak: "I reckon she done it to save Dell."

Lily felt tears of relief welling up into her eyes. Still holding the rifle cautiously, Matt climbed up out of the wash. He looked directly at the sheriff and said harshly: "You've got Dell Tillman. You've got his confession and two witnesses to back it up. What are you going to do about it?"

The sheriff said—"I'll bring Tillman in."—but Lily knew he was lying. There was a shiftiness about the sheriff's eyes that betrayed him. Lily looked at the man and felt a reluctant pity. Alf Polk was in a squeeze, all right. He was desperately in love with Elaine. He had probably talked to Elaine before leaving town, and Lily guessed she had put the same price on herself

for Alf that she had for Matt, that price being Dell's freedom.

It was a price Alf was prepared to pay. The shiftiness of his eyes told Lily that. The sheriff turned toward the posse. "Go on back to town. I won't need any help bringing in Tillman."

That was apparently the final tip-off to Matt, if one had been needed. He walked over to the wash and got his horse. He rode back and looked at Lily with warmth in his eyes. "Go with them. I'll see you later."

"What are you going to do?"

"I've got to see Kip. And Lily?"

"What, Matt?"

"I owe you more than I can ever pay. I owe you my life."

She was wordless, but her eyes told him many things. Her eyes promised him the world if he came back to her. And her eyes told him that she knew what he intended to do, but her lips were silent.

Her smile was tight, perhaps a little sad, for she knew he was going into worse danger now than any before.

Matt wheeled his horse and rode away at a gallop. He turned at the crest and looked back. Lily had not moved. She was watching him, and she lifted a hand in farewell, as he rode down the slope and dropped from sight.

Riding out, he had pointed his horse toward Rocking H. But as soon as he dropped out of sight, he veered away from that course and took a direct one toward Tillman's DT. Three miles lay between the turn-off and Tillman's ranch. Matt covered them in less than twenty minutes.

He rode in openly, and his eyes were quick to spot the horses, sweated and unsaddled, which had been turned into the corral to cool.

Matt rode up to the bunkhouse and quickly swung down from his horse. He called: "Olaf!"

Olaf Skjerik came to the door, hulking, blond, cold as ice,

and scowling.

Matt said: "Call out your crew."

"Get the hell out of here, before somethin' happens to you. I still remember that clout you gave me on the neck."

"You'll get more than that before I'm through."

Olaf started toward him, and the crew came pouring out of the bunkhouse behind Olaf.

Matt said sharply: "Hold it!"

There was that in his stance, and in his expression, which stopped Olaf as though he had walked into a wall. He looked disturbed for a moment, then gathered himself for a rush.

Matt said evenly: "The jig's up, Olaf. Tillman's confessed to the sheriff that you and he murdered Dan and my brothers. He's confessed that they weren't moving DT stock but their own. Somebody saw what happened that day. Kip Reynolds was along."

He grinned at Olaf's open-mouthed amazement, fully aware that when the big foreman recovered from it he'd be as dangerous as a grizzly bear.

Matt went on: "Joe Furness got a look at some of the brands that day. And you told Joe you'd kill him if he told, didn't you? Well, you won't be killing anyone, Olaf. Because you'll be in jail. And when you are, Joe will tell what he knows."

Behind Olaf he noticed Joe Furness slipping furtively away, and let him go because this suited his purpose.

He said: "The other two will probably be let off pretty easy. They thought what they were doing was on the level, if not quite legal. But you knew better."

Olaf's mouth snapped shut, and his eyes glittered. His huge body seemed to go tense and still.

Matt said swiftly: "The rest of you stay out of this and you'll be all right. Olaf's figuring on making a play. He knows he's hooked. Stay out of it, hear?"

Matt knew his own skill with a gun. He knew himself to be fairly fast. He knew as well that Olaf Skjerik, for all his bulk, was supposed to have a lightning draw. It was probably what Tillman had hired him for.

Behind Olaf, Tillman's crew scrambled aside, leaving open space behind the foreman. To right and left they scattered, and Matt knew that unless they stayed neutral, he was finished.

But he faced this as he had faced everything else since he had alighted from the train at Granada—with fatalistic concern. Whatever the outcome of this battle, he had won. He clung to that belief. He had won vengeance for Dan and Frankie and Will, and he had cleared the Hurst name.

But remembering Lily Kibben, he knew he did not want to die.

Olaf fell into a half crouch, his hand but an inch from the butt of his gun.

Matt glued his eyes to the foreman's, and waited. The waiting grew long and intolerable and at last he said hoarsely: "Scared, Olaf? You've got guts enough to hang an innocent man, but have you got guts enough to face one who can shoot back?"

Olaf's face twitched. And Matt heard the slightest of movements behind him and off to one side, toward the house.

He felt cold sweat break over his body. He dared not turn his head for even a lightning glance. Then he heard Tillman's choked, painful laugh. Saw Olaf's cruel expression of triumph.

Matt said, never taking his eyes from Olaf's face: "How did you get away from Rocking H, Dell? Didn't Alf leave a guard over you?"

Tillman chuckled, though the sound was filled with pain. Tillman said thickly: "Only Kip. He got careless and I slugged him."

There was a momentary silence. Matt's hands were sweating and he knew the palms would be slick as he grabbed for his gun. But he dared not try to wipe them on the sides of his pants. He dared not move those hands. For when he did, bullets would come at him.

Tillman growled: "Take him, Olaf."

Olaf's hand sped for his gun. It cleared leather, the hammer coming back.

As though from far away, Matt heard a scream—a woman's scream. But there was no time for thought of anything but this. No time to look up, no time to be surprised or even to think.

A man's movements became automatic under the prod of mortal danger. Matt realized that his gun was in his hand without quite remembering how it got there. On the heels of the click of Olaf's gun hammer came that of Matt's. And quickly following that, Tillman's, unseen off there to Matt's side.

Matt's gun bucked against his palm, and Olaf's shot came like an echo. Matt felt a savage blow in his thigh. It was if a horse had kicked it out from under him. He drove backward, falling, and, at that precise instant, Tillman's gun spoke, the bullet cutting air where Matt had stood but a split second before.

Rolling, forgetting Olaf for the moment, Matt brought his gun from beneath his body and snapped a swift shot at Tillman's crouching form.

Tillman never got off a second shot. He dropped his gun and clawed at his throat an instant before he collapsed.

Matt heard the woman's screaming plainer now. He forced himself up to a sitting position and looked at Olaf.

The foreman stood solidly on his feet, his gun smoking in his hand. But he didn't fire again. He stood that way for what seemed an eternity, and at last began to sway like a giant pine in a gale.

A red spot on his shirt front began to spread. Matt struggled up to his knees, sick and dizzy with the pain in his thigh. He felt the softness of Lily as she crouched beside him, unmindful of the danger that yet lurked in Olaf Skjerik's gun.

Matt started to push her away, stopped as he saw Olaf collapse onto the hard-packed snow. He turned a little, realizing that her arms were around him, that her tear-dampened face was pressed very close against his own.

He kept saying over and over: "Lily, I told you to go to town. I told you to go to town."

He tasted her lips, salty with tears but unbelievably sweet for all of that. When she could speak, she murmured shakily: "Matt, I belong with you. I belong with you."

He murmured—"Yes."—but it took her second kiss to convince him that he was not delirious, that he wasn't dreaming this. The pain of the flesh wound in his thigh disappeared and he felt as though he were ten feet tall.

ACKNOWLEDGMENTS

"Gun This Man Down" first appeared in *Dime Western* (3/54). Copyright © 1954 by Popular Publications, Inc. Copyright © renewed 1982 by Catherine C. Patten. Copyright © 2010 by Frances A. Henry for restored material.

ABOUT THE AUTHOR

Lewis B. Patten wrote more than ninety Western novels in thirty years, and three of them won Spur Awards from the Western Writers of America, and the author received the Golden Saddleman Award. Indeed, this points up the most remarkable aspect of his work: not that there is so much of it, but that so much of it is so fine. Patten was born in Denver, Colorado, and served in the U.S. Navy, 1933-1937. He was educated at the University of Denver during the war years and became an auditor for the Colorado Department of Revenue during the 1940s. It was in this period that he began contributing significantly to Western pulp magazines, fiction that was from the beginning fresh and unique and revealed Patten's lifelong concern with the sociological and psychological affects of group psychology on the frontier. He became a professional writer at the time of his first novel, *Massacre at White River* (1952). The dominant theme in much of his fiction is the notion of justice, and its opposite, injustice. In his first novel it has to do with exploitation of the Ute Indians, but as he matured as a writer he explored this theme with significant and poignant detail in small towns throughout the early West. Crimes, such as rape or lynching, are often at the center of his stories. When the values embodied in these small towns are examined closely, they are found to be wanting. Conformity is always easier than taking a stand. Yet, in Patten's view of the American West, there is usually a man or a woman who refuses to conform. Among his finest titles, always a difficult choice, are surely *Death of a Gunfighter* (1968), *A Death in Indian Wells* (1970), and *The Law at Cottonwood* (1978). No less noteworthy are his previous Five Star Westerns, *Tincup in the Storm Country, Trail to Vicksburg, Death Rides the Denver Stage, The Woman at Ox-Yoke,* and *Ride the Red Trail.* His next Five Star Western will be *Hang Him High.*